# THE LEGACY SERIES

# SERIES TITLES

*Broken Heart Syndrome*
Anne Colwell

*The Mexican Messiah: A Novella & Stories*
Jay Kauffmann

*Never Stop Exiting*
Michael Hopkins

*The Hopefuls*
Elizabeth Oness

*Close to a Flame*
Colleen Alles

*American Animism*
Jamey Gallagher

*Keeping What's Best Left Kept Secret*
David Ricchiute

*Soaked*
Toby LeBlanc

*The Path of Totality*
Marie Zhuikov

*Shocker in Gloomtown*
Dan Libman

*The Continental Divide*
Bob Johnson

*The Three Devils and Other Stories*
William Luvaas

*The Correct Response*
Manfred Gabriel

*Welcome Back to the World: A Novella & Stories*
Rob Davidson

*Greyhound Cowboy and Other Stories*
Ken Post

*Close Call*
Kim Suhr

*The Waterman*
Gary Schanbacher

*Signs of the Imminent Apocalypse and Other Stories*
Heidi Bell

*What We Might Become*
Sara Reish Desmond

*The Silver State Stories*
Michael Darcher

*An Instinct for Movement*
Michael Mattes

*The Machine We Trust*
Tim Conrad

*Gridlock*
Brett Biebel

*Salt Folk*
Ryan Habermeyer

*The Commission of Inquiry*
Patrick Nevins

*Maximum Speed*
Kevin Clouther

*Reach Her in This Light*
Jane Curtis

*The Spirit in My Shoes*
John Michael Cummings

*The Effects of Urban Renewal on Mid-Century America and Other Crime Stories*
Jeff Esterholm

*What Makes You Think You're Supposed to Feel Better*
Jody Hobbs Hesler

*Fugitive Daydreams*
Leah McCormack

*Hoist House: A Novella & Stories*
Jenny Robertson

*Finding the Bones: Stories & A Novella*
Nikki Kallio

*Self-Defense*
Corey Mertes

*Where Are Your People From?*
James B. De Monte

*Sometimes Creek*
Steve Fox

*The Plagues*
Joe Baumann

"Anne Colwell's *Broken Heart Syndrome* uses layers and multiple lenses to skillfully illuminate all the weight we carry in an imperfect life: grief, love, disappointment, and joy. Colwell has a poet's eye for exquisite details that pinpoint who we are, and her characters look out for one another in small, beautiful ways. You will want to keep returning to these words."

—ETHAN JOELLA
author of *The Same Bright Stars*

"Through all the heartbreak and loss, the mistakes and disappointments, I was cheering for every last one of the characters in Anne Colwell's debut story collection, *Broken Heart Syndrome*, to make it. Doctors and nurses, patients and their loved ones, all are drawn with such care that they truly come alive on the page. The hospital around which these stories revolve is fertile ground for the dramatic, and Colwell lets her tales unfold with rare compassion and honesty. It's a big cast of characters, but I fell in love with them all."

—CLIFFORD GARSTANG
author of *What the Zhang Boys Know*

# BROKEN HEART SYNDROME

STORIES

## ANNE COLWELL

CORNERSTONE PRESS
UNIVERSITY OF WISCONSIN-STEVENS POINT

Cornerstone Press, Stevens Point, Wisconsin 54481
Copyright © 2025 Anne Colwell
www.uwsp.edu/cornerstone

Printed in the United States of America by
Point Print and Design Studio, Stevens Point, Wisconsin

Library of Congress Control Number: 2025934057
ISBN: 978-1-960329-81-3



Cornerstone Press titles are produced in courses and internships offered by the Department of English at the University of Wisconsin–Stevens Point.

DIRECTOR & PUBLISHER
Dr. Ross K. Tangedal

EXECUTIVE EDITORS
Jeff Snowbarger, Freesia McKee

EDITORIAL DIRECTOR
Brett Hill

SENIOR EDITOR
Ellie Atkinson

PRESS STAFF
Kimberly Janesch, Sam Zajkowski, Cora Bender, Anicka Montgomery, Sophie McPherson, Madison Schultz, Autumn Vine, Ava Willett

*For my mom and dad,*
*Mary Anne and Tom Colwell*

# STORIES

# NINE MONTHS

After Jeff died, the dog started freaking her out.

Bowtie was Jeff's dog, though they'd picked him out at the shelter together. Bowtie was his dog the way the Sierra Club and Greenpeace mail was his and not hers, even if her name was above the address.

They'd gone to the Milford SPCA eight years ago on a cold morning in March. There had been frost on the windshield, and Jeff had scraped it off with a flat branch when he couldn't find the scraper. She'd sat in the car with a travel mug of coffee in her hands, the seat cold against her legs, even through her jeans, and she watched the slender blue lines he made and watched the crystals that formed around them.

He threw the stick, opened the driver's side door, and slid in beside her, rubbing his chapped red hands and turning up the windshield defroster. He looked at her sidelong, wary. She wanted to say something, but all the words she could think of seemed as thin and cold as the lines etched on the glass in front of her. He reached over and squeezed her knee, then put the car in reverse and looked over his shoulder.

She remembered every detail because they'd fought the night before. Later Jeff called it a debate. But it had always felt like a fight when she thought of that night, and all these years later, she could feel it again, the tightness inside her and the ache between her eyes. The fight ended only because she'd run out of arguments and conceded, finally, that overpopulation was a dire problem, and they wouldn't bring children into this world.

Then she'd gone into the bathroom and shut the door and sat down on the toilet and cried as quietly as she could.

She hadn't meant to talk about it at all. It was the dog that started it. They had decided to go to the SPCA and adopt the dog the next morning and, while they were making dinner, they'd started talking about names. Jeff was standing on the other side of the butcher block, chopping a Vidalia onion in a quick, decisive flurry of small strokes.

Since his death, she thought about his hands a lot, pictured them on the steering wheel of the car, running up her legs. She wanted to see his hands again; she missed them. She catalogued all the small scars in her head so there would never be a day when she would forget. The long line on the pad of his left thumb where he'd sliced it open cleaning a fish, the spatter of small red acid burns on the middle fingers of his left hand from an experiment gone wrong in his inorganic chemistry class, the mangled nail on his right pinky from closing his hand in the car door as a kid. His fingers were strong and short and stout. He told her once that, when he was a boy, his piano teacher had held his hands in hers, sniffed, and called them "butcher's hands." They'd laughed about it, lying in their bed all those years later, when he mocked the teacher's German accent and love of Wagner.

They'd met when she'd taken her first-grade class to the College of Marine Studies for a field trip. He'd been recruited to talk to them about the huge sea worms he was studying. All the girls shrieked when he pulled the thing out of the tank—a foot long and pink, with legs like a centipede, and a gaping toothed mouth. She'd taken a step back herself and then laughed and shushed the kids. He looked up at her apologetically and mouthed, "I'm sorry." She liked him right away, his quiet eyes and his mortification at having caused such a fuss. She liked the way he held eye contact with the kids as he answered their questions, the way he bent to their level as he showed them the impossible creatures in the huge tanks, the striped sea robin with its fins like bird wings and the golden tilefish's enormous pop eyes. His kind voice. His easy laugh.

THEY HAD BEEN MARRIED just a few months when they stayed the weekend with friends of his who had a sweet German shepherd named Buster. Both Sylvie and Jeff fell in love with him, and the dog took to them, too, sleeping at the foot of the bed in the guest room and following Jeff wherever he went. Sylvie watched the gentle way Jeff stroked the dog's ears and ran his hand down the smooth flank. She hadn't grown up with dogs, but Jeff had, and she watched with a kind of awe as she saw how easily he connected with Buster. She could see the boy he'd been as he threw the ball high, shouted as Buster leaped for it, as they ran in circles around each other in the yard.

On the drive home, they had decided to get a dog of their own, a shepherd maybe, or a mix, a rescue. She'd always wanted one when she'd been a girl, but her mother had been too ill. Her "sick headaches," as the family called them, meant she had to keep the television low, play music softly. A dog, there was no place for that in her house—the barking, playing, tearing around. With Jeff, she'd made a different kind of home with music playing while the coffee brewed, friends stopping by for serious conversations—climate change, politics, books. Bright paintings, loud laughter, a barking dog.

That's why it seemed almost unbelievable to Sylvie that naming the dog could have been the spark that touched off their first real married fight. It started innocently enough—cooking dinner, talking about what happened in the day, about work, going to the SPCA the next morning. She still wore the clothes she'd taught in, a Snow White sticker on her sweater. The winter afternoons were just starting to get longer, and as they talked, Sylvie looked out the window over the sink and noticed the last of the light sinking behind the bare trees.

She'd suggested calling the dog something like Oliver or Phoebe, and Jeff had scoffed.

"You can't call a dog a person name. What if we meet someone named Oliver and become friends?"

"Lots of dogs have people names."

"Yeah, but those dogs are owned by people who say the dog is their children's 'brother.' We will never, and I swear this to you now, call our dog our 'fur baby.' That's just sad."

Sylvie flashed to Jeff romping across the grass with Buster and laughed. "That's what everyone says before they get a dog," she said.

"Why don't we just call it Mutt?" Jeff said.

Sylvie stopped stirring the simmering tomatoes and turned around to look at him. "That ... is singularly unimaginative! Are you going to call our son Boy, Tarzan?" She'd been pleased with her wit and turned back to the pot again, but when he started talking, the wistfulness in his voice made her turn and look at him.

"If we ever had a boy—which we won't—I'd want to name him Martin after my dad. I know that sounds weird, since I never knew him. But my dad's half my DNA and some part of me wants another chance to know him." He slid the knife through his fingers and shook off the stray bits of onion. "It's crazy," he said. "Martin!" and he waved the knife in the air like he was scattering the sound of the name.

Sylvie, who'd thought for the two years they'd dated that she understood and accepted Jeff never wanting children, felt as if she'd suddenly been able to hear after years of being deaf. They would have children after all! It was there in his voice. She looked down at the wooden spoon she was holding, the red stain already drying into the grain. She pictured their son, suddenly, completely; she saw his quiet gray eyes like Jeff's, his hair, thick and dark as hers. She imagined he'd have Jeff's curiosity, his athletic grace, his sweetness. She fell in love with him, instantly.

"I want that boy," she said, astounded at her own words, astounded at how much she wanted him. "I want a son, Jeff. A boy named Martin."

She watched as the expression on Jeff's face changed, as the open door closed, and he put the knife down slowly. "We've talked about this," he said. "We've talked about this forever, from the very beginning."

He was right, too. They'd had these conversations over and over in the two years they'd known each other. Jeff had wanted her to make sure she didn't want children, and she'd reassured him over and over. "I work with children all day long," she'd said. "I have enough children in my life." Or "We can spend time with children still. We'll volunteer at the Boys and Girls Club or coach sports or something." She'd loved their life together, their late dinners with friends, sitting up until two talking, their long Saturday hikes with no obligations, no timetable.

But she'd never imagined a real child with a real name. Martin, a boy that Jeff would love. That she would love.

Suddenly, standing in the kitchen, she felt confused and overwhelmed and angry. Angry at Jeff for having opened the door a crack and then shutting it again. Angry at herself. Had she even thought this through? Had she really asked herself if she'd wanted kids, or did she just agree?

Sylvie looked down at the sticker on her sweater. "Look," she finally said, her voice tight with tears, "other people who care about the environment have children. They must have reasons that make sense to them. Maybe we could just… keep the subject open."

Jeff blew out an exasperated breath. "I knew this would happen," he said. "Damn it, Sylvie!" He braced himself against the butcher block on his arms and didn't look up at her.

"I didn't know," Sylvie said. "I didn't know it until this minute."

"I haven't changed my mind, Sylvie, and I'm not going to. I told you this as soon as we started getting serious. You know I did!"

"I know, but . . ."

He picked up both fists and brought them down hard enough that Sylvie jumped. "This is the exact fucking moment I was trying to avoid!"

Sylvie moved toward him, but he circled away. "I just see what a good father you would be. I see . . . I see how it could be with the three of us. With Martin."

"There's no Martin! There's never going to be a Martin!" Jeff fighting to keep his voice level, pulling out bits and pieces of conversations they'd had in the past, words she'd once agreed with. He looked at her, pleading. "How could I be a good father if my decision contributes to destroying the planet for that child?"

"Our child," Sylvie said quietly.

LATER, SITTING IN THE BATHROOM, dabbing her face with toilet paper, she thought of the nights they lay on the couch in the basement apartment he'd lived in when he was finishing his PhD, how he'd talk to her about the whales he'd seen in British Columbia and the old growth forests, the golden eagles. "Humans!" he said. "Before we're done, we'll kill it all, cover it over." And she'd agreed, too. She'd never seen what he'd seen, but she knew that everything was more crowded and polluted than it used to be. He changed her, knowing him, listening to him. She drove less, recycled, thought about what she bought before she bought it. She had believed that she agreed with him about everything, that he'd made her a better person.

But sitting in the bathroom, she realized with a dawning sickness that since she'd met Jeff, she hadn't taken her own beliefs, her own priorities, seriously enough. That she'd never deeply considered what he had asked of her, was asking of her now, what the price for being with him would be. It stunned her. She looked up into the mirror over the sink at her tear-stained face. How could she have accepted his view of the world so easily and not, even for a moment, fought it?

BOWTIE WAS A MUTT. The sign on his cage at the SPCA said he was a shepherd/black lab mix, but he'd never grown very tall, and his coat was soft. He had white socks on his front paws and a patch of white fur at his neck shaped like a bow tie. Sylvia thought it made him look strangely formal, like a sad man dressed for a big party he didn't want to go to. Sylvie could still see the way he'd looked that March morning, the way his head lifted from his front paws when they stopped in front of his cage. The way he'd leaned his head into Jeff's hand as it reached through the bars and the way he'd closed his eyes when Jeff scratched his ears. Jeff was so gentle with him, so kind.

She'd loved the dog from the first, too. It was impossible not to love him with his trusting chocolate eyes and his silly cocked ears. The woman at the shelter said he'd had a rough time of it in his first year. He'd been taken away from people who neglected him, kept him chained up outside, went away for days at a time leaving the dog with no water or food.

"The neighbors called it in," she said, shaking her head. "Can you imagine?"

On the way home in the car, Sylvie sat in the back and the dog put his head in her lap and fell asleep. She kept stroking the soft fur between his ears and felt sleepy herself, lulled by the heat and the motion and the calm that was stealing over her.

SINCE JEFF HAD DIED, the dog moped around the house most of the time, looking behind doors and into closets, heaving a big sigh when he lay down on the brown dog bed in the corner of their bedroom.

Sylvie had googled "what do dogs do when their owners die" and read that they grieve in some of the same ways humans do, that they sometimes refused to eat or play. But what she hadn't read on any of the sites was what Bowtie was doing on quiet afternoons or in the middle of the night, the way he would get up and wag his tail, stare at something in the middle distance, bark a little, or pull his head down between his front paws as he'd always done when Jeff scratched between his ears. Bowtie would stand expectantly by the closet at night, just as he had when Jeff was getting undressed at the end of the day. Sometimes he'd even offer his paw and then sit, his only trick. Jeff loved it. "Paw?" he'd say. "Sit." And then Bowtie would jump up, his forelegs on Jeff's thighs or belly. It always made Sylvie laugh.

Now when he did it, Sylvie stared at the emptiness in front of the dog and went still. She felt a maelstrom of joy, stupid hope, and terrible, choking grief.

"There's no one there, Bo." She said it once and then again to convince herself.

JEFF HAD TAKEN the dog everywhere: he rode shotgun when Jeff went to the store, came to Jeff's mother's house for dinner, even ran with Jeff in the park. Sylvie was a runner, too, but she and Jeff rarely ran together. Once she called him on it, laughing: "You like running with the dog more than running with me!"

"You can't keep up." Jeff put his arm around her shoulders. "Bo can."

He called the dog "Bo" and "Bobo" and "Baby Bo" and lavished it with affection. The dog slept at the bottom of their bed always with his head on Jeff's ankles or feet.

She'd wake often now in the middle of the night and find Bo there again, though that side of the bed was empty.

They'd gotten Bo in March, and as the weather started to warm up, Jeff would come home from working at the lab and spend an hour before dinner playing with him, tossing the frisbee or a ball for Bo to fetch. One night in July, she'd watched out the window as he threw a pink rubber ball and Bowtie brought it back, dropping it at his feet, jumping around him in anticipation. The warm butterscotch light poured through the trees and already, in the woods across the street, the dark was settling in. She said the words "playing catch" out loud and imagined, just for a second, baseball mitts and watching Jeff play catch with Martin, the little boy they wouldn't have.

It wasn't that she regretted or resented the dog. It was just this: in the days that followed that March morning when Bowtie came into their lives, Sylvie started running another narrative in her head, a narrative that was loose and disjointed and impossible, one that would suddenly come out of nowhere, one she never told anyone and barely admitted to herself. One in which Martin was born that cold March morning, and she'd imagine sometimes what he might be doing had he ever "arrived," what their lives might be like. She'd imagined Christmas mornings holding the baby. The little blue cake they'd bought him and put on his highchair for his first birthday. How he'd have rubbed it in his face. The picture of him on his first day of first grade. She'd been dreaming that story for eight years when Jeff died.


SYLVIE LAY IN BED watching the dog out of the corner of her eye. "Bo! Come on, Bo! Come up on the bed with me!" She patted her hand on the beige comforter beside her.

But the dog stayed still, looking with great intensity at the closet and whining in the back of his throat.

Bowtie did this now two or three times a week, sometimes more, whined at the closet door in the middle of the night, or right at bedtime. Barked at nothing. Tracked something moving through the room when Sylvie couldn't see anything. Now she stared at the closet, too. She imagined Jeff not the way she'd seen him in the emergency room after the accident—the bruises blooming around his ear and down his jaw and neck, the line where they'd shaved his head—but whole and well, stepping out of the closet and explaining that it had all been a misunderstanding. Sometimes she'd dream she saw him riding his bike or walking down the street, and she'd suddenly be so happy.

Then she'd wake up and remember. He'd been riding his bike the way he always had, every Thursday night, leaving from Bill's Cycle Shop and riding over the Indian River bridge and back with the guys. The driver had been an old woman; the EMTs said she'd had a heart attack.

The ER nurses had tried to clean Jeff up. She could see that they'd rubbed off blood from around his mouth and nose. She was grateful they'd done that. She was grateful, too, that they'd asked her if she wanted to see him, that the tall doctor with the long braid had held her hand when she opened the door. But she wasn't sure she'd made the right decision. Now sometimes, when she thought of Jeff's face, it was this image that came to her—the bruises, his lips blue, his closed eyes made of wax. And always in these moments when Bowtie was whining at the closet, she imagined opening the door and seeing Jeff in pain. The grief of it, imagining him hurt and needing her at the end, would double her over. Once or twice, she'd gotten up and turned on every light in the house and gone to the closet, flung open the door, and burst into tears when the smell of his clothes poured over her.

The only suit he owned, the one he'd worn to funerals and weddings, she'd buried him in. There were a couple of sport jackets, white dress shirts, flannel plaids, the denim jacket.

His running shoes sat in the corner next to the cowboy boots she gave him their last Christmas. She remembered how he put them on and did a two-step to make her laugh. The clothes held the lines of his body, and Sylvie missed him with a physical pain that coursed along her nerves for hours after.

"Get rid of the clothes." That was what Brian told her when she'd finally had the guts to tell him about Bowtie. He was Jeff's best friend, another scientist, and she knew he wouldn't take this seriously and she welcomed his scorn. She got together with him for lunch about once a month. She had been working herself up to telling him about Bowtie. She knew it would be like telling Jeff. Jeff would have laughed at her, too, told her she was not reasoning clearly, was letting emotion rule.

She woke in the quiet sunlight of a late spring day and gathered up green bags and boxes. She'd do it. She'd box up what could be donated and throw the rest away. She opened the closet. Bowtie took out one of Jeff's shoes and carried it to the middle of the floor. Then he got the other and put it down beside the first and looked up to about the place where Jeff's head would have been, conjuring him. A wave of grief broke over her. Sylvie's knees gave and she sat down on the foot of the bed and looked up to where Bo was looking, squeezing the balled green trash bag tight in her hands.

"Jeff," she said. "Jeff. Jeff." She said it over and over again, as though saying it could make him present. The dog went back and forth, back and forth between Sylvie and the place where Jeff wasn't standing, wagging his tail, sitting, giving his paw. The afternoon light splashed on the floor around the shoes. Shadows from the trees moved over the carpet like gray hands. She sat there a long time until Bowtie broke the spell, darting back out into the hallway and down the stairs, barking at something he heard passing in the street. She looked down at the shoes, the cowboy boot folded over itself, the running shoe on its side, then she felt calm, different, as though she had decided something that she couldn't put a name to. She felt the dog had conjured something of Jeff inside that circle of shoes. Sylvie took a long breath and held out her hand toward where Jeff might have been.

She put back the shoes and boxes, shoved the bags under the bed.

THE NEXT WEEK, she and Brian sat at a table in the window of Peace o' Pizza, squinting against the afternoon sun. The campus was quiet because exams were over. The last school year Jeff would ever know was done. She watched as students walked slowly by the window, not rushing off to classes or parties.  She wondered if he'd taught any of them, if his students missed him. Brian chewed his crust thoughtfully while she sipped her diet Coke.

"Did you get rid of the clothes?" he said, gently.

She had known he was going to ask. She knew it was time; three seasons had passed. She looked down at her salad in the white carton on her lap. She'd lost ten pounds since Jeff died. She meant to eat; she tried. She'd get hungry and fix herself some food but when she sat down to look at it, her stomach revolted.

"No," she told Brian. "Not yet." She took off her sunglasses and rubbed them with the hem of her shirt, looking away. "I'm not ready," she said. "We're still grieving."

"We're?" Brian looked at her until she looked back. "We're? You and the dog? Sylvie? You and the dog?"

Her throat tightened, but she swallowed, willed the bile back down. She would not be sick. She would not cry. She heard, in the field behind them, the voice of a boy calling, "Dad." She wondered if the boy was really there or if she had imagined him.

# HOW FAR THEY TRAVEL

The sand hissed around him as the January wind lifted it into the dunes. He curled his cold fingers inside his gloves. It was ten o'clock in the morning and the sun, a white disk behind the screen of clouds, gave no warmth. The bay shone flat and metallic in the cold.

He still felt the tightness around his temples from the beers and shots the night before. Around 5:30 that morning, he'd opened his eyes to a dark room he didn't recognize. He had to close them again and lie still until he could focus the picture, blurry images coming clear. He remembered her mouth, red with lipstick and the way the lipstick stained the ends of the brown filters in the ashtray. The whole night came back. A nurse. He'd met her on Chemistry.com. They'd gone for drinks at the Summerhouse. Tina? Tricia? All night he'd wanted to call her Theresa. Something about her was very Theresa-ish.

He'd woken up beside her, moved a little, pulling the pillow out from under his arm, and felt her move, too. When her phone chirped, she turned on a little pink lamp beside the bed.

There on the wall in front of him were six-inch high wooden letters on a tiny shelf—T – I – N – A—all woven with vines and roses. He laughed out loud.

"What's funny?" Her voice sounded like she was underwater. He rolled toward her, and she moved her dark hair out of her eyes with one hand and wet her cracked lips. Brian could smell the cigarette smoke in her hair and see a shadow of last night's bright red ghosting the edges of her mouth.

"Nothing," he said, "I'm just happy. I always wake up happy." He almost never woke up happy, but how could you tell a woman you'd slept with that you remembered her name only because it was there on the wall?

"You're not hungover? Because I'm, you know, still feeling it a little myself." She rolled away from him, pulling up the sheet to cover herself. As she moved, the sheets brought the smell of sex and perfume, of his own body in the bed. "I've got to get to work," she said. "My shift starts at seven o'clock." She held up her phone and squinted at it. "What's your number?"

When he told her, she dialed it, and he could hear his phone buzz in the pocket of his jeans that were somewhere on the floor by the foot of the bed.

"There. Now you've got mine, too." She leaned over and kissed his forehead, and he could see her breasts under the sheet and the scar below her collarbone that he had almost asked her about last night. "I had fun," she said. "I'm going to go shower and get ready. Happy snail hunting!"

At some point in the night, he'd told her he had to track snails in the morning, that he had to get up early so he wouldn't miss the tide.

"You're full of shit," she had said. "You're messin' with me now." She grabbed a napkin from the stack in front of him and he noticed that her fingernails were torn and uneven and he wondered if she bit them. The band in the corner started a bad, slow cover of Clapton's "Layla."

"No, really. It's my job. Well, part of my job."

"You chase snails?"

"Not chase, track. We test them for parasites and then put numbers on them and measure how big they grow and try to figure out how far they travel."

"How far can a snail go?"

*More than a thousand miles depending on the snail's lifespan,* he thought. But he'd learned long ago not to go "full nerd" on the first date, and he didn't want to talk about work.

Tina kept a skeptical half smile ready just in case the snails were a joke, just in case she was being played. He watched her watch him from behind that lop-sided smile as he spoke, and he thought they'd never work out, though she wasn't bad looking, and she seemed nice enough. But she had those flat, Southern Delaware "A's," and it already irritated him, and he knew then; he knew her type. The type who didn't put up with him for long—practical, scarred, wary. These were the kind of women he tended to meet on Chemistry, nurses and teachers who'd been divorced, maybe two or three times. Women with children and stories. They were so guarded. He wanted something spontaneous, something wild; he wanted abandon. On Match or Tinder, he met the same women, just a little younger, maybe not married yet, or only once. Their profiles said they were "looking for fun and maybe more." He once made Jeff laugh by saying that they should all say "looking for more and maybe fun."

"If any woman writes that," Jeff said, "you marry her! Don't even hesitate! You propose on the first date, you hear me?" Lying there watching Tina get out of bed, he thought about calling Jeff. He wanted to tell him about Tina, to tell him that he'd been hopeful and that the hope made the disappointment bitter. The knowledge that he couldn't ever talk to Jeff again pressed against his eyes.

Brian was thirty-seven, and he'd never been married or lived with anyone. He'd had a couple of relationships that made it a year, and his last one, Amelia, made it six—or was it seven?—months. That was it. All of this—the websites, the coffee dates, the sex (or lack of it), the drinks, the dark rooms, strange kids and dogs, the ringing phones he didn't want to answer—it wore him thin, exhausted him. He didn't remember when that had started to happen. But after waking up with Tina, he wanted nothing more to do with any of it. A wave of nausea rose from his gut to his throat, and he swallowed it back down. Not for the first time, he thought, *I'm done.*

Sometimes he imagined his ideal woman, waking up with her or looking over at her on the passenger side of the car or holding hands in line for a movie. In most of his fantasies, she looked a little like his high school girl friend—dark-haired and coltish, with small high breasts and no hips. But she wasn't silly or giggly like Julie had been. His ideal woman was . . . well, she was smart, like Jeff's sister, Regina. He could talk to her about the melting polar ice caps or marine parasites, but she wasn't a scientist either or she didn't need to be. He'd rather she were something free-spirited, like a musician or a sculptor.

"So, you want a tall, dark hippie?" Sylvie had teased him when he described his perfect woman. That was a few months back, right after Jeff died. He'd come over to check on her.

When he called, she'd sounded good, but when she opened the door, she looked like hell. She had on a stained sweatshirt and flannel pants. Her eyes looked dull and there was a line where her hair color was growing out. He asked her how she was, but she just shook her head and held up her hand and dropped it in her lap, then sat in silence.

Brian sat on the couch beside her, stared at the pictures along the mantel. Though he'd seen them all before, seen them every time he'd been there, he hadn't noticed them the way he did now that Jeff was gone.

There was one of Sylvie and Jeff standing close, the Eiffel Tower just visible in the background. Beside that, their wedding photo—Jeff had been sunburned and he had a goofy smile. Brian stood beside him in the tux that had pinched him under the arms that whole night. The picture to the left made Brian's stomach tighten—Jeff and Sylvie, Regina and him, glowing in the flash, some summer night years ago. A bonfire on the beach. Jeff had his arm around Sylvie and his sister, and Brian had leaned in at the last minute over Regina's shoulder.

How the hell could he have slept with his best friend's sister on the night of the funeral? He felt the shame sting his eyes every time he thought of it. The shame and the grief.

He wondered if Sylvie knew. Regina and Sylvie had always been close. Women told each other everything, didn't they? What the fuck had he been thinking?

"I'm a mess today," Sylvie said. "You honestly don't have to stay."

Brian reached out to touch her arm, but his hand settled awkwardly on the couch between them. "I'll just hang out awhile if it's okay with you," he said. "I miss him, too. I—" He couldn't finish the sentence. *I'm destroyed*, he thought, but he couldn't say it.

A cloud passed over the sun outside and the fall light disappeared from Sylvie's face. "You and Amelia? You guys aren't back together or anything are you? I just ask because she sent me a card. Did you know that? And she came through the receiving line at the funeral. I don't know if she stayed. I remember she was very kind when I spoke to her. I have no earthly idea what she said to me, but I remember it was nice."

*She doesn't know then*, Brian thought. "No, we're not back together," he said. "She'd never have me back even if I wanted to go there. I burned that bridge. Burned it good!" He made an exploding sound and stretched open his hands and eyes.

Sylvie laughed. "Bullshit. She'd take you back, and you know it."

They were quiet a moment and then Sylvie said, "So, have you seen Regina? Since the funeral, I mean?"

THE FUNERAL, A MEMORIAL service really, had been in the community room in the Marine Studies Building. Everyone sat in the gray plastic chairs in front of the podium like they were in some sad and formal seminar while people got up to talk about Jeff.

"It will be a kind of a loose thing," Sylvie had told him beforehand. "You can talk if you want. It's completely up to you."

Brian had labored over a paragraph that he read quickly and without looking up until the last sentence. When he got to the final word, his throat was so dry he could hardly swallow. He raised his eyes. He saw Sylvie and Regina sitting next to each other. Sylvie was tiny and looked smaller sitting next to Regina. Sylvie nodded at him tearfully, but Regina wasn't crying. She stared into the middle distance, like she was concentrating on the motes of dust in the air. She looked stricken and furious. Like him, she'd bury the sadness. She shifted her eyes for a breath and met his and then looked away again. She smoothed the black skirt across her broad thighs.

As he moved to sit down, he wished he'd been sitting next to her. Regina would have understood what he'd just tried to say. She was the only person who could really understand him in that room.

"It's the weirdest thing" Sylvie was saying. "I thought I knew something about grief, when I lost my mom, my nephew. But I . . . I never imagined. Maybe no one can . . . I miss the dumbest things, hearing him talking to Bowtie in another room, the way he loved to make breakfast, celebrated flipping the egg with no spatula. I just . . ." Sylvie lifted her hands and let them fall.

"I saw my mom two days after the funeral," he said. "She took me out to lunch to tell me she was sorry I lost Jeff, and it was okay if I was gay." He'd been imagining telling Sylvie this story, had known it would make her laugh. He'd wanted to call Regina and laugh with her about it, too, but he hadn't been able to. He wished again he'd never slept with her.

Sylvie's eyes widened. "No!"

"Yup. She told me she would still love me and even though she was Catholic, she didn't care at all, and it would be just fine." Brian watched as Sylvie tried to move through the waves of grief toward him.

"That's very . . . progressive and liberal-minded of her."

"You have no idea. I assured her I wasn't, and she asked what the problem was in finding a nice girl then."

"What is the problem?"

Brian stood up. "Mind if I grab a beer or some tea or something?"

"You can't get out of it that easily." Sylvie swiped under her eyes with the sleeve of the sweatshirt, and Brian saw her hand shaking.

He'd felt the question buzzing around him like it electrified the air. What was the problem? In college, he'd wondered himself if he were gay because the best times he could remember weren't with the women he dated but with friends, hanging out. He'd even asked Jeff about it. Jeff said, "Do you want to sleep with guys? Imagine having a loving relationship with a man?" When Brian shook his head, Jeff said, "Then you aren't gay. Case closed."

As Brian walked behind the couch, he looked at the picture of Regina again, her eyes slanted up toward his face. "I'm like my snails," he joked. "That's what Jeff used to say. I want a shell and my whole house on my back so I can just move when I'm ready." He flashed back to Jeff saying this, to the two of them in the diner, the late-night breakfast, and

Brian felt his throat constrict. He cursed himself silently and took a long pull from the beer to swallow it down.

Then, Brian heard something and turned, and for half a heartbeat, he imagined he saw Jeff coming through the door. That had been happening for a week. Some part of his brain kept forgetting Jeff was dead and he'd see him—walking down the hallway at work or on the beach in the morning. Once he thought he saw him going into Starbucks, and he couldn't let it go until he went in the store and looked at the face of the guy in the blue jacket that was almost like the one Jeff wore. Just like those other times, Brian blinked hard, and the world readjusted itself. Every time it happened, he'd get furious after; he knew it was bullshit, magical thinking. He focused on the empty hall, the white door, looked down and saw the dog pawing at the door to go out. He felt disoriented, lightheaded. He wondered if this were happening to Regina, too.

Sylvie opened the door, and the dog scooted around her and out into the yard.

"You're not a snail," Sylvie said, and she came and stood beside him behind the couch. They stared at the pictures on the mantel. "Jeff," she laughed, "could say some stupid shit. You know that."

"But I knew what he meant," Brian said, "I'm crawling along right at the line, looking for something that doesn't exist in the world. Something I'll never find."

HE'D BEGGED OFF for dinner, stopped on his way home and picked up pork fried rice. The cold air knifed through him. He wanted to tell the waiter who brought his food to the counter, "My best friend just died," but he knew that would be weird.

Alone in the car in the dark, he thought about Sylvie's question again, about his mother thinking he was gay, about the funeral, about Regina's laugh as they talked in her dark bedroom, about all of it. He thought about the last time he saw Jeff, an ordinary day, saying goodbye to his retreating back as he disappeared into the hallway.

He thought again, this is how you end up alone, and the thought hollowed him out. What are you waiting for? He'd meet someone and feel such excitement, believe for days or sometimes weeks that she was the one, maybe even believe he loved her, like he had with Amelia. He'd save mementoes from their dates—playbills and movie tickets—he'd plan elaborate excursions. They were touched by his care, his morning phone calls, his spotlight attention when they spoke. He wrote funny emails, self-deprecating, called out this "mad scientist" persona. But he wasn't running a game; he believed the things he said. He got to be the wonderful guy they saw, his best self. He liked who he was with them. He'd even let himself imagine a future sometimes. The whole dream: coming home to a family, tucking the kids in at night.

But then the moment would come. The one he couldn't come back from. A kind of exhaustion, a disorientation like his life had suddenly turned into a telescope and he was looking through it the wrong way, everything small, distant, meaningless. He never knew exactly what triggered it. Sometimes it was a repeated phrase that he couldn't stand or a gesture, something simple. Jocelyn said, "Totally, totally," over and over again. Marjorie tossed her hair every time she laughed and left her lipstick-stained wine glass wherever she'd been sitting. Sometimes it was nothing obvious, nothing he could put his finger on, just that he suddenly would rather sit on his couch and watch TV than try.

When he got home with his Chinese food, he collapsed onto the couch and grabbed the remote, but he couldn't concentrate. Couldn't care. He clicked the TV off again and sat in the quiet.

It occurred to him that he should have coffee with Regina, talk it out. Apologize and explain. Get it all behind them.

He decided he'd call her midmorning, when she'd be at work, right in the middle of things, so it wouldn't be a long phone call, and she couldn't get emotional. They'd go out for coffee.

IT TOOK HER THREE RINGS to answer and when she said hello her voice sounded preoccupied.

"Hey," he said, "I'm sorry to bother you at work. I was just . . . wondering if maybe you wanted to get together."

For a beat she didn't say anything, and he could hear the sounds of the store behind her and the sound of the filter running in the snail tank. Then she said, "Sure. Where do you want to meet?"

"How about Café a Go Go on the Avenue?"

"Oh no!" she laughed. "No way in hell."

"What?"

"Brian, you are not breaking up with me. I'm not going to Café a Go Go so you can give me your 'It's not you, it's me' speech or any version of it. Don't be an ass. Nothing's changed. We slept together. Whatever. Nothing's changed."

When he hung up with Regina, he felt better, but also worse, unsettled. Like he was more transparent and more cliché than he ever realized, and something else, something he couldn't identify.

He looked over at the empty stool where Jeff always used to sit when they were working together in the lab. He stared at his phone in his hand. He would never speak to him again. Never. It seemed like he understood that word for the first time.

THE NEXT DAY AFTER WORK, he got on the Chemistry site again. She's out there somewhere. He told himself, *You won't find her if you don't look.* He put the laptop on the kitchen counter, opened the screen, and logged in. This was the part that had always excited him before, seeing their pictures, the music they liked, their favorite food, imagining where he might take them—the restaurants, community theater, maybe later, a get-away—all the ways he could make them like him, love him. This time, though, their smiles depressed him, their cliché activities—long walks and movies, their hometowns and favorite books. Everything felt cardboard.

But he forced himself to do it, to look, to type his usual first message—nice, casual, noncommittal, studied. He closed the laptop and went to the refrigerator. Leftovers, a single bottle of beer, a withered lemon from God only knew when. Brian grabbed the beer, pulled an open bag of chips from the cabinet over the oven. He imagined writing, "Hi [fill in the blank], I'm eating stale chips and drinking my last beer. My best friend died, and my life may or may not be coming off the rails. Want to get together and get to know each other?"

The thought made him laugh out loud, but the laugh felt hollow.

By the next morning, they'd all replied.

Three first dates—an awkward coffee, a rushed lunch in a diner, and the one night with Tina. She'd sent him a cheery little text about how fun it was getting to know him with a kissy emoji. He was done. Done. He'd never find anyone, and he didn't care. He didn't care if he ever slept with anyone again. He didn't care if he died alone choking on pork fried rice or if he became one of the crazy, lonely scientists he'd met at conferences who could only talk about bats or parasites or leaf mold.

BRIAN PUSHED THE TOE of his boot into the soft sand and turned over some rocks and bits of shell. The salt smell across the bay flashed to the smell of sex and cigarette smoke from the night before. Brian thought of the scar above Tina's collar bone he hadn't asked about and felt the terrible loneliness of it all tighten across his shoulders. The beach stretched out in front of him, and as he walked the tideline, the gulls lifted and settled and lifted, always just in front of him. He pulled his knit hat down closer over his ears.

Then, out of the corner of his eye, he caught a flash of the red nail polish that he and Jeff used to mark the snails. They usually found marked snails every couple of weeks, but since Jeff's death, Brian had seen none. He bent to pick the snail up, filled suddenly with joy, inexplicable joy. This was one Jeff had marked, and he imagined Jeff walking beside the water months ago and lifting this same snail. He felt for a moment like he did when he thought he saw Jeff, a sizzle in his hands and behind his eyes like waking from a dream. The small life in his hand felt like a bridge, a connection. Brian blew out a breath, pulled the notepad from his pocket and looked at the tiny white number lacquered to the shell: fifty-six.

But when he flipped to the right page, he saw the snail wasn't one of Jeff's. It was one of his. He'd marked it two months ago. "Of course," he said, and he swallowed the grief that rose in his throat. He took off his glove and wrote, "10:27 a.m." and "tideline" with the golf pencil he carried in his pocket, and then he set the snail down at the water's edge again and watched the brown shell disappearing alone under the brown sand.

# BROKEN HEART SYNDROME

Tancredi runs me through the patients, what tests we're waiting on, the man with the possible stroke whose wife's drunk in the waiting room, the woman in the ambulance that passed me on the road.

"It's Mrs. Shipley," he says. "The usual drill. She wants to leave AMA, says she's old and just wants to be left alone to die. Doesn't remember that she was here last week. She's looking for you but doesn't know it."

I look over to the far side of the trauma unit and scan the red plastic chairs for Sylvie. Mrs. Shipley's looking for me and doesn't know it. I'm looking for Sylvie and don't know why.

I do it at the start of every shift. I look at the place where she sat weeks ago, where I held her hand until her friends and family came. She isn't there, of course. Why would she want to hang out in the place where her husband died? What is it that I expect? She'll be here because it's a Friday, and he died on a Friday? She'll be here because I will her to be? And why do I want this?

Plenty of patients come back to say thank you or to ask questions they thought of only later. Even those who lost someone, like Sylvie, will come back sometimes and ask to see me. They want to know if the person suffered, if there was anything else they should have done. They bring flowers, candy, and one time, a lasagna. Delicious! Of course, it's not like being an oncologist or some specialty like that. There's an oncologist here whose patient gave her a car. Not that HR let her keep it, but still . . . a car. Some have brought me books they thought I might like, or even a picture of the person who died so I could see what they looked like before the accident or the sickness, or just when they were young. One woman brought me in a picture of her mother from 1951 wearing a Marilyn Monroe-style white bathing suit and posing on the fishing pier.

"You wouldn't know it from what you saw," she had said, "but she was a beach girl. She lived here all her life, and until the stroke, she walked down by the water almost every morning."

Early in med school, on my first rotation in the ER, the attending told us never to follow-up with our patients. Not to blow one of the best things about emergency medicine—you don't wake up worrying, never on call, never trying to solve the unsolvable puzzle.

"I'm not saying 'tube 'em and move 'em,'" he said. "I'm just saying you can care a lot when they're sitting in your ER bay. Do your best, then let it go."

At first, it was one of the things I loved about emergency medicine. I could show up for people in the worst moments of their lives; I could help. Then I moved on. I rarely wondered what happened because there was always another crisis. But lately, well . . . I don't know what's come over me. Sylvie wasn't even my patient. Her husband was, and he died before he got to me. What is it that feels unfinished? What do I want? Need?

I run my hand down my braid, still wet from the shower and now cold. Tina walks by with another nurse; they're having a hushed conversation and pushing two IV poles. I ask Tancredi about Mrs. Shipley's vitals.

He's showing me the screen. "BP and pulse are elevated, but that's probably because she's here. The home aid brought her in again—chest pain, dizziness. Her daughter will be in Rehoboth tomorrow. So . . ." He hands me the iPad and puts his feet up on the desk.

"You better get out of here before the fun starts," I joke. It's not that I really think it will be crazy, but Tancredi's department head so the whole staff calms down as soon as he walks out the door.

"It was quiet today," he says. "But there's a fresh pot of coffee just in case."

Any time there's an ER on TV, everyone runs flat out through their whole shift—eight straight hours of multi-vehicle collisions and gunshot wounds. Everyone screaming diagnoses over the top of moving gurneys. Lawsuits everywhere. No one ever eats pizza in the break room or tells a joke. Summer here is busy, but now, in the off-season, it's the odd weekend where the crowds come, Jazz Fest or The Sea Witch Parade. Mostly, we get the usual suspects: chest pain, fainting, broken bones, UTIs, cuts and contusions. That's who's here tonight. I walk down the line of bays and hear the alarm going off on an IV, the rasp of someone with asthma trying to breathe.

I find Mrs. Shipley in the third bay, crying. She doesn't remember that she knows me, but she does, knows I'm here on Fridays. She's seen me every weekend since August. She was here the night Sylvie's husband died. When I say, "It's good to see you, Ada," she keeps talking like I've said nothing. She's reciting the litany—the three C-sections, breast cancer, four surgeries on a broken foot, then she curses in Czech.

"*Hovno*," she says. "I've no one left here. My husband died. I want to see him again. I'm ready."

"When did your husband die?"

"Yesterday."

I reach for her hand, and she lets me hold it. Her skin is dry and loose. I can feel the bones under it.

I've always remembered hands, noticed rings, watches, nail extensions, red knuckles, the callouses of contractors and carpenters. The night Sylvie's husband died, her freckled hand held onto the curtain as she stared at his body under the white sheet, just his bruised and shaved head showing. She wasn't wearing a wedding ring. She whispered her name to me when I asked, as though she might wake the man who lay there in front of her. She held her brown hair back in the other hand, her knuckles white. Under her lifted arm, I saw the two small holes in the armpit of the threadbare blue T-shirt. Something so intimate about these two holes.

Her husband. Massive trauma from a bike accident. He was gone when he came in. I did nothing. There was nothing *to* do. That's what I told her when she thanked me. He was gone before the ambulance ever got to him. Gone on impact. I wonder if she finds it consoling. I would.

It's what I hope for when I imagine dying. One blistering moment and then nothing, or whatever comes after breath, after thought. I don't know what that might be because I never had my mother's faith. Czech Catholic, part of the underground church during the Soviet regime, she has believed all her life, believed with the guns in her face.

Mrs. Shipley's Czech, like my mother, and though she doesn't remember that I tell her about my mother from week to week, some part of her knows. Her daughter lives somewhere out West. Something in Mrs. Shipley's heart has softened the lines between me and her daughter, blurred the picture.

A man laughs too loudly in the next bay and a woman's voice shushes him. Maybe I'm in the wrong specialty now. Patients are getting attached to me. I'm getting attached to . . . well, she was never my patient.

When I move my hand down to her wrist, Mrs. Shipley's pulse is thready and too quick, faster than when they took it in triage. I press "nurse call" and hear the quiet doorbell sound in the hallway. We've worked hard over the last few years to limit the noise. When I first started, every machine had an alarm, and every day was a cacophony of high-pitched squeals and constant loud beeping. I ask Mrs. Shipley to take off her sweater.

She pulls it tighter across her chest. "I'm cold," she says. "Just let me go home. I don't know why that girl always brings me in."

"The aid said you complained of chest pain."

"Not chest," Mrs. Shipley says. "It's here." She puts her hand over her breast like she's pledging allegiance. "It's my heart. My heart hurts because my husband died yesterday."

*Two years ago*, I think, but I don't say it. I wonder if she has felt like it was yesterday every day since he passed. I move my stethoscope around her back, but the cardigan is too thick.

Tina slips through the curtains. "Are you feeling any better, Mrs. Shipley?"

"Ada," she says. "You can call me Ada." She cocks her head at me and points. "This one says it's her mother's name." She lets one corner of her mouth turn up. "It's not your mother's name, too, is it?"

"You remembered!" I drop the stethoscope from her back and come around to face her. "I didn't tell you this time. You remembered that you share my mother's name."

Her eyes blur like she's running over and over an impossible puzzle. "I don't know what you mean. You did tell me. You just told me."

Tina looks at me full of sympathy and shakes her head.

"Of course," I say. "Of course, I did. We need to get that sweater . . ."

Tina gets a blanket for Mrs. Shipley and we get the sweater off and I start to auscultate, listening to her heart and lungs.

Mrs. Shipley begins to sing a Czech lullaby.

I let go of the stethoscope and whisper-sing the words with her. "*Hajej, dadej, nynej.*" My mother used to sing it. Something about little angels.

The muscles in her shoulders relax. "You are Czech," she says.

I say what I always do, what I did last week: "My mother is Czech, like you. My father was a diplomat. I lived there growing up. You have to stop singing for a little bit, Mrs. Shipley, so I can listen." I lift her shirt in front and put the bell of the stethoscope in the middle of a constellation of small dark moles. I don't like the cellophane wrapper sound when she breathes.

"ECG," I say, and Tina slips out again.

Mrs. Shipley tries to stand up and follow Tina. "I want to leave, too," she says.

"Let's chat for a little bit until Tina comes back. When did you leave Czechoslovakia?" This conversation always calms her. It has an easy rhythm, details she likes to rehearse—her father's sweater with the fraying cuffs, her red suitcase, the yellow door, the names of her friends. When she says "my father," she smiles like she can see his face, like she is fifteen again, and he's handing her the red suitcase.

"In 1967. Right before the Prague Spring, the Soviet invasion. My father was a diplomat."

"Mine too," I say.

"I don't—to this day—I don't know how he got us out, how he got us here."

"How old were you?" I ask it even though I can see her fifteen-year-old face clearly. I can scrape away the years in my imagination and see her walking out the yellow door of that house into a new life.

"Fifteen. He said we were going on a long trip. He pulled my red suitcase out of the closet, and I noticed how frayed the cuffs of his sweater were. Only take what you really need, he said. We can't pack too much. That's what he said. He said, 'Do you understand, *broučku?*'"

*Broučku.* This is new. I search for the word a moment, my Czech rusty. "Beetle? He called you beetle?"

"Little beetle. A family nickname. I had black, black hair. I wanted my father to think that I understood what was happening, why we were leaving, that I was grown up, a woman. But I wasn't. I didn't. I didn't understand at all."

Then she jumps back into the usual details, the flow. "I didn't know we'd never see that house or any of my friends—Berta, Katka, Lucie. Berta and Katka had freckles; they were sisters. Lucie had a space between her front teeth. The yellow door of our house—that's the last thing I remember. I looked back at it before we left."

I stare at her. Her color isn't good. She's breathing fast. What made her change the story? What made her switch tracks, remember something new? "Tell me about the nickname," I say. "I want to hear more about your family calling you *broučku.*"

But then, Tina comes back in with the ECG machine. "I'm going to help you into a gown," she says, "and Dr. Kriz will step out and be back in a moment."

WE STEP OUTSIDE AND Tina says, "The ambulance just brought in a young guy. Fell through a window. His blood alcohol's through the roof. I called up to the OR, but you better take a look."

I tell her to do the blood work on Mrs. Shipley after she's finished with the ECG.

Face first. Deep lacerations on his jaw and neck, on his arms, but it's his eyes—swollen shut with the glass in them. We get the ophthalmologist, the OR; we get him upstairs.

Mrs. Shipley's ECG comes back abnormal—left bundle branch block, a prolonged QT interval. Weird. *We'll be admitting her again*, I think. We've done it twice before. I know she won't like that, and I'm already thinking about how I'll go upstairs and visit her in CCU, follow her as she recovers.

What's wrong with me? I've never thought to ask her how her husband died. I wonder if it was his heart, quick and shocking, or if it was something she had time to adjust to, like cancer. Milan. I think his name was Milan.

What was Sylvie's husband's name? I search around the corners of my mind for it. I know it's there. He went out the door healthy, to do something healthy, and never came back. Is that more heartbreaking than watching someone slip away breath by breath?

Heartbreaking. If Milan really had died yesterday, Mrs. Shipley's ECG would make me think of takotsubo cardio-myopathy broken heart syndrome. But it's been two years, not two months. It can't be that. If it were Sylvie with that ECG, I would suspect, but—

But what if yesterday doesn't mean the same thing to everyone? What if, because she thinks he died yesterday, that's the truth. True for her body, for her cortisol, for her heart?

The syndrome is named takotsubo because the heart looks like the pot Japanese fishermen use to catch octopus—bell-shaped, bigger at the bottom.

I look in on the patient with asthma, then go back to check on Mrs. Shipley. Why did she remember my mother's name? Why add the "little beetle" detail?

Tina has an IV set up. Mrs. Shipley is singing another song. At first, I think it's a lullaby, then a Czech folk song, then no—I listen again and realize that it's the Czech cover of Air Supply's "Lost in Love." I laugh and sing the English lyrics along with Mrs. Shipley's Czech. *"You know you can't fool me, / I've been loving you too long./ It started so easy."*

The song came out when I was eleven. Nela would play it and whisper along. As I listen again to Mrs. Shipley's heart, Nela's face swims into memory. Another heartbreak. She was a ballerina. She lived in my bedroom at the embassy for three weeks after her husband was shot, slept on the bottom bunk with the stuffed animals. We kept the blinds drawn. She could never speak because we knew the residence was bugged, but sometimes she would hum and stretch her impossibly long legs out against the wall.

Prague. The dark cars driving past every hour, the click and whir when I picked up the phone. If my parents missed the curfew, I spent the night alone with the servants. My father warned, "They are watching, Zsu Zsu. Anyone you talk to might be trying to hurt you."

Nela wrote on a little white tablet, and she cried in the barest whisper into her pillow every night until my father found a way to get her out. She had long dark hair and dark eyes and her feet were fascinating and horrifying, like the hooves of some impossible animal, a unicorn maybe, or a centaur.

Mrs. Shipley has stopped singing and is settled against the pillow. "Are you having trouble breathing?" I ask.

She says, "Is your mother from Prague?"

Her pulse is faster now, and her breathing worries me. "Close to it. A city called Cesky Krumlov."

"I know that place!" she says. "Milan and I visited there. That's a fairy tale place. The red-roofed houses and the bridges over the Vltava River. Beautiful."

Mrs. Shipley starts to shiver, and I tuck the blanket closer around her and look at the monitor. Something feels off, but I can't put my finger on it.

"You must miss Czechoslovakia," I say, but she says no, that she misses only people.

"Everyone's gone now but me," she says, and I think of the list of friends in her story, and it makes me suddenly sad.

Two silent men snuck Nela and her dying husband into our house, up through a secret door in the floor. I was the first to see them. I started to call out for my father, but his hand came around and clamped over my mouth. Her husband must have bled out through an artery. His face had that ashen color, and he was shivering.

Hospitals are cold. Sylvie shivered the night her husband died, and we wrapped her in blankets while she waited for her friends and family to arrive. Later, someone brought her a blue hoodie. She'd stopped crying by then and sat staring at nothing. I've tried to imagine what she was thinking.

"I should just go home," she said aloud, but she looked at the bay where he'd been and didn't move.

My mother hated that the ballerina was in our house, in my room. She and my father had arguments about it with their eyes—my mother's, furious and protective; my father's, pleading. Sometimes he'd hold his thumb and forefinger an inch apart to say, "It's just a little while." Sometimes my mother cried at night and my father would hold her and whisper, "*Snesl bych ti modré z nebe*" – I would take the blue from the sky for you.

Mrs. Shipley moans low in her throat and closes her eyes. A sheen of sweat breaks out along her upper lip and forehead. I look at the monitor. "We need to get you upstairs," I say as I press the nurse call button.

All those days, I watched the ballerina move through our house like some silent, long-limbed insect. Thin, so thin, arms and legs like sailor's rope, all those nights sleeping just above her on the top bunk, looking down at her dark head buried in the white pillow. I didn't know then what heartbreak was, how it came in one phone call, in one breath, how it could rise through a trapdoor in the floor and come into your room.

"I don't want to go upstairs yet," Mrs. Shipley says. Her eyes look like a girl's, like I've told her she has to go to bed. "I thought we'd have more time."

"We will," I tell her, and I know it's true. We will admit her to CCU, and I will go up before I leave in the morning and check on her, even though I will fight with myself about it.

The cardiology people will run all the tests again, and none of them will show us any more than they did the last time. Because her heart is broken, but not in the way we can fix. Her heart is broken like Sylvie's, like Nela's, like everyone's. Like mine. I think of the people I've loved and lost. I hear again my father whisper to my mother, "*Snesl bych ti modré z nebe*" – I would take the blue from the sky for you. Tomorrow, we'll discharge her and tell her she's fine, and she'll be back the next week and the next because her confusion is wiser than our machines and diagnoses. Because she understands more than I do about the heart.

# THE JUDGE

At sunset, the ocean flattened and silvered like a worn coin. Helene wanted to sit down on the wooden steps and watch the day darken. Or, better, go home and go to bed. That was what she really wanted. No one she had to talk to, no words she had to say. But she forced her gaze back to the people passing on the boardwalk. It won't be a busy night, she told herself. It was three weeks into September, the shoulder season, as her boss at Obie's called it, and the crowds had thinned. The people who remained—older, calmer—weren't too interested in happy hour at a boardwalk bar.

When a young guy caught her eye, she forced a smile and recited her pitch, "Two-dollar pitchers, and a special on wings. You should come in!"

He turned his head, kept walking.

Helene lifted her eyes to the horizon again, looked at the red clouds far out on the ocean. She thought about what was beyond that line: Seville, Paris, places she'd never been, places Peter had told her about years ago. Peter was dying. She'd seen him in ICU that morning; she'd watched his chest—so thin now—lift in pain as the oxygen pumped through the tube and into his lungs, and she knew he couldn't do this on his own, couldn't breathe, couldn't speak. She thought, he's already gone. She'd touched his hand but couldn't hold it. A tube taped into the vein. His fingers gauzed and wrapped for reasons she didn't understand. She put her index finger on the thin, purple skin beside his thumb.

She'd been to see him almost every day for the last two weeks, more than she had in some previous years. She'd try to sneak in when no one else was around, off times—dinner, early in the morning. She asked the nurses about his condition every time she went, though she knew they weren't allowed to give her any information. She asked just to look in their eyes when they said it. To look at their faces. The nurse she'd spoken to that morning held her gaze and touched her arm. She said, "I can't say, but . . . the family has been here most of the night, his wife, everyone. Do you understand?"

Helene imagined Peter's wife as she'd first seen her at the Christmas party twenty years ago: a blonde, bird-like woman almost lost behind the huge poinsettia she carried. Helene had thought then that Peter sought Helene out because she was so different from Kat—dark, and curvy, and almost as tall as Peter. He'd told her that Kat had eaten only peanut butter and ramen noodles all through law school, where they'd met. That she vacuumed when she was angry. If he heard the vacuum as he came down the walk, he said, he wanted to turn around and get back in the car. Helene remembered other things. Kat loved chocolate-covered pretzels and old movies. She never gained weight. That it was Kat who'd started calling their oldest son, Peter John, P.J. and that Peter had cringed at the nickname at first. They'd honeymooned in Paris—a city Peter loved, and Kat hated much to his dismay.

"Maybe you and I will go to Paris someday. I think you'd appreciate the beauty of it." It was one of the few times Peter had ever mentioned anything about future plans with Helene. She remembered looking out the car window into the rainy parking lot as the words hung there between them. She had no illusions about what she was, what they were.

The lights blinked on at the edge of the boardwalk and Helene got out the gray tub full of silverware and napkins and started to roll them into table settings, tucking the napkins carefully, top and bottom. A group of people walked by, and she called out, "Great wings and two-dollar pitchers!" and the woman called back, "We don't need any pictures, thanks."

Helene had started as a social worker in family court right out of college—a children's welfare advocate. Peter was a judge. Forty-five to her twenty-four. The affair lasted almost a year. The earliest days seemed dizzy, spiked with possibility—the September afternoon when he first kissed her in the park at lunch, the weekend trip to the quaint town on the Chesapeake Bay where sailboats docked at the end of every street, the metal clips of their unfurled masts clapping against the poles. When Helene thought of the girl she was then, she rolled her eyes at the cliché. It wasn't surprising to her when she remembered it now that the dizzy feeling hadn't lasted long, not for either of them.

Mostly, they talked. It was the part Helene liked best about being with him. There were afternoons where they'd gotten undressed and then just talked until it was almost time to go, their sex a strange afterthought, a rushed obligation beside the hours of conversation. He'd lie beside her in the Murphy bed in her walk-up efficiency, or in some anonymous hotel room, and he'd throw an arm or leg over her and say, "Look!" marveling at his white against her brown. They'd talk, analyze everything, the bailiff who'd just had her seventh child, Illinois vs. Gates, the Dred Scott Decision, the best pizza, the books they'd pass back and forth, their families. Her father was Puerto Rican and her mother Greek, and Peter used to sing her name. "Helene Martín Lopez!"

She told him about growing up on Kimmey Street in Georgetown, about the houses where four or five families—brothers, sisters, cousins—all lived crammed together, sleeping on any open floor space, everyone working different shifts at the chicken plant. Her mother cooked for half the neighborhood, passing out tostones and papa relleños that her grandmother had taught her to make. Her grandmother "prescribed" Puerto Rican herbal remedies, explaining to Helene the properties of tulsi berry tea, saw palmetto, yarrow leaf. Sometimes Helene went on house calls with her grandmother. It wasn't, Helene told Peter, too different from the visits she made as a child advocate for the court, the distraught families, the poverty; assessing the strength of the malady, trying to help cure it.

Peter always said he had no childhood stories to match hers; "All vanilla," he said—an only child, wealthy, alcoholic parents, boarding schools, loneliness. He'd always dreamed himself a family like hers.

"Helene Martin Lopez!" Sometimes he'd sing her name that way when he saw her in the hallway, or even in his chambers. It was their joke—a thrill, telling the secret in public. She'd wondered since how many people knew and realized that the answer was everyone.

Peter had encouraged her to go back to school, get a master's degree, go to law school. "You're too smart to do this every day," he'd said. "You're going to burn out. You know that, right? This isn't a job you can stay in."

"I'm too nice to be a lawyer," she'd tell him, and he'd laugh. But she thought it was true. She'd listen to lawyers in court—the smooth lies, making the words say one thing and sound like another. She'd watch them yelling into their cellphones on the steps before they went in, their tense walks, narrow eyes. They all said they hated their jobs. She never saw anything she wanted for herself. Even Peter could be that way sometimes—tense, wound tight and hard.

But she wasn't like most of the other professional child advocates either, the starry-eyed do-gooders who'd cry over every file and have to quit in a couple of months, or the jaded women—they were mostly women—who'd seen everything, who felt nothing. She believed she was better at the job than anyone she worked with. She believed that she had some kind of almost infallible radar for which children needed to be moved out and which could stay. She thought maybe it was the way she grew up. She'd visited neighbors with her grandmother, knowing drug dealers, gang members who were her friends' fathers and brothers. She knew that life mixed everything, that everyone did things to survive, but that didn't make them bad people, or people who couldn't love their children. Like the friend's father who'd cooked meth in the garage and used the money to send all four of his kids to college.

But she also grew up Puerto Rican Catholic, believing in evil, knowing that some people could be taken by a lie, turned into demons. She'd seen that too—a man who'd beaten his son with a chain, parents who'd locked their daughter in a closet as soon as she came home from school so they could get high and fuck whoever they wanted.  She never said it to anyone, but Helene believed that she could understand the people whose lives she walked into. She couldn't explain it to her coworkers, to Peter, so she'd just say, "These are my people," and she meant it.

ON THE BOARDWALK, a mother walked by with an infant in a soft carrier at her chest and toddler by the hand. All she could see of the baby was the pink hat. The wind off the water had made their faces red and the mother kept her other hand wrapped around the back of the baby's neck to keep her warm. Every three or four steps the little boy tugged hard on his mother's arm and jumped as high as he could. "Up, up, and away!" his mother said. "Superman!"

Though it was so many years since she'd done it for a living, Helene had never lost the habit of looking closely at the families she saw, assessing—when they came into the restaurant, in stores, wherever she saw them. It had been worse these last few weeks, with Peter dying, and though she tried to resist, tried to keep afloat on the tide of her own days, she kept going under, getting drawn back into the life—the lives—she had left and back to the strong light of all those judgments.

Seeing this mother on the boardwalk, this happy family, Helene thought of the brochure they used to pass out to people who came into the office wanting to volunteer as child welfare advocates. Well-meaning people. Some who'd been involved with the system themselves, who'd gotten custody of grandchildren, who'd been rescued from their own parents. In the picture on the front of the brochure, a volunteer advocate in a smart blue pantsuit and tortoise-shell glasses sat with a clipboard in her lap in a well-appointed living room full of light and tasteful knickknacks. Across from her sat two white, well-dressed parents in their thirties holding a fat, healthy, smiling baby girl between them. The baby reached a soft pink hand across to grab the volunteer advocate's finger.

Everyone in the office laughed about the picture.

"Oh, for Christ's sake," they'd say, "That child had a college fund in utero."

"Wait, Stacy doesn't have all the Dr. Seuss books yet? After two baby showers? I think we need to look into removal."

It wasn't funny, really, because the picture was so far from what they saw. Children raised in a house with no plumbing, mold growing on the food in the broken refrigerator. A four-year-old boy beaten with the heel of a shoe. The neglected infant with the bloated stomach and arms like matchsticks. Both parents on crack and the kids alone for days. Helene had wondered how someone, some administrator some-where, had looked at that brochure, that image, and thought, "Yes." She imagined pigeonholing the photographer and giving him (she always imagined it was a him) an extended and specific tour of the truth, the lives that some children lived.

The boardwalk darkened, but Helene didn't want to go inside. A breeze kicked up. The sand hissed across the boards and the last of the summer trash skittered from light post to light post. She felt like Peter's death was dragging her into the past, making her question everything. She couldn't understand why she didn't just shake it off. The affair, the Tyler case, leaving social work, all of that happened years and years ago. Peter wasn't even someone she'd thought about often, more of an obligation, the occasional lunch or coffee every couple of months. She only heard about him being in the hospital because a mutual friend from those days had come into the restaurant, had mentioned it in passing. Why did she feel so pulled apart by something she'd left so long ago?

PETER HAD BEEN RIGHT, of course. She couldn't stay in the job. But it was the way she left. One case ended it: the State vs. Tyler. A case that she and Peter had shared, a case they'd both misjudged. It ended their affair and her career, and tied them together, incredibly, inexplicably, for these twenty years. Jesse Tyler. The boy's brown eyes held hers and she was standing in that doorway again, then kneeling in front of him, taking the open ketchup packet from his hand, the only thing he'd eaten for three days.

She shook her head hard as she always did when he came into her mind, tried to force herself back to the present. She thought of Peter in the hospital bed the last time she'd been there. The horrible rattle of his breath. Helene felt the convulsion rise from her stomach to her throat, thought she might be sick. The smell from that apartment twenty years ago floated out from the open door of the restaurant, rose from the ocean, unclean and terrifying—grease, sweat, the sweet awful edge of decay. The pink blanket over April Tyler's dead body in the crib. Jesse holding April's limp hand, saying, "She's a good baby. She doesn't cry at all," as Helene picked up the corner of the blanket.

Helene had to see Peter. She couldn't breathe or the smell would kill her. She had to see Peter. She pushed the gray tub of place settings back under the hostess station, and pulled out her purse, and then she left. A thought passed like a cloud that she would probably be fired, and she imagined the angry face of her manager, John, as she fumbled in her purse for the keys, struggling to breathe. She'd had lots of waitressing jobs; she was great at it. She'd find another. The lights slid over the parked cars; the cold air constricted her lungs. She walked faster so no one from the restaurant would see her, walked faster so that smell wouldn't settle around her, inside her. "I'll find another," she said out loud, tasting the cold fresh in the words.

HELENE AND PETER HAD TALKED about the Tyler case only once, right after it happened, after Helene had resigned, after she'd ignored Peter's calls for a week, hidden in her apartment when he banged on the door downstairs and called her name.

He'd come back two days later. She'd watched him through the window, crossing the street in a steady rain. He'd looked like a lawyer, tense and determined, his salt and pepper hair neatly cut, his gray suit spattered with wet spots. When she opened the door, his face softened.

"It's not your fault," he said. He'd tried to hug her then, but she turned away.

"*Our* fault," she'd said. "It is our fault. That baby would be alive now if we hadn't . . . *I* hadn't—" And though she couldn't see Peter's eyes, she could imagine the look in them. Helene walked away from him, curled herself into the corner by the window, her shoulder against the cold glass.

"This sort of thing . . . it's a numbers game. You can't save them all. You just can't. No one can, no matter how hard you try. You did your best. Sandra Tyler looked like she was recovering. She'd done everything you could have asked her to do to get those kids back. She'd gotten a good job, a place to live. No one would've made another decision."

Helene shifted so her forehead was against the cool window. She couldn't look at him. "Would you have looked at the case harder if it weren't me in that court room? You were—"

"No."

"—biased because of our affair, because I talked you into putting those kids back in that situation and you believed me because we were fucking, and I was biased because . . ." Helene picked up each of the possibilities one after another like a row of knives, "because I'm so arrogant, because Sandra Tyler was white, because I wasn't careful, because I should have visited more than once a week, because—" As much as she tried, she couldn't articulate the thing she really felt, that it had happened because of the totality of who she'd been up to that point, of who she was, not just her arrogance and carelessness, but her belief in her own goodness.

Peter stood two feet from her with his hand out, but he didn't touch her. "No," he said. "No. No. No. Please, Helene, don't run away, don't let this grief kill everything, cover everything. Let this go. You've got to let this go."

SANDRA TYLER TURNED A PLAIN gold wedding band around and around on her finger while she spoke to Helene. Her nails were short and manicured, the nail polish clear, her arms and hands freckled. They sat in the living room of the halfway house where Sandra was staying, among the hodgepodge of ancient, donated furniture—the torn green couch, the coffee table scarred with white rings and burned at one edge. Sandra had served six months in prison for possession and endangering the welfare of her children, but as soon as she'd gotten out, she'd contacted the court about getting them back.

Helene watched her turn the wedding band. "Are your kids with your husband now?"

"Not exactly," she said. "They're with him but living with his mother. My mother-in-law. Well, she'll be my *former* mother-in-law soon. He's divorcing me."

Helene waited for the narrative she expected, whatever version of it would appear. Sometimes they didn't want the kids back at all. But Sandra clearly did. So Helene expected to hear it was her husband's fault. He'd cheated on her, given her the drugs, was addicted himself. And her mother-in-law would be an awful woman who hated Sandra and hated the children.

"Is your husband the father of both children?" Helene checked her sheet. "Both Jesse and April?"

"He is," Sandra said, "and he's a good dad. He and his mom are taking good care of them. I just . . . I guess I think they need me. And I need them. I miss them." When she started to cry, it wasn't the loud hysterics that Helene had grown used to. Sandra's tears felt real, each spilling one-at-a-time from eyes that tried to blink them back.

"It's all my fault," Sandra said. "It started after April was born. It was a hard labor and after, well, they put me on painkillers, and I got addicted right away. In days. Maybe it's because my dad was an alcoholic. I don't know. But when they wouldn't give me anymore, I started stealing painkillers from the people I worked for. I'm a visiting nurse. I *was* a nurse, I mean, but . . ." She pointed to the file folder. "You probably know that."

Helene nodded. "That's when you started shooting heroin?"

Sandra buried her face in her hands, then she looked up at Helene and whispered, "I can't believe I did it. That I could have done it. You don't understand. I love my husband, and I love my kids. I would never do anything to . . . I want them back. I want them all back. I don't know how I'm going to do it, but I know I can. I can fight for them. I love them."

Helene did what they'd been told never to do. She believed her. She reached out her hand and held Sandra Tyler's. Instead of saying that she'd look into it and see what she could do, Helene said what she'd been told not to say, "I'll help you."

PETER CALLED HER AGAIN the next day and the next, but she wouldn't answer. She slept until late afternoon, ate little. Sometimes she'd wake up already crying, or she'd wake from terrible dreams to the sound of her own voice calling words she didn't understand. She'd thought she might be losing it and thought she should answer when Peter called and tell him, or call someone, her parents, one of the women at work, one of her friends, but then the anger would burn through her, hot in her chest and hands, anger at herself, at Peter, at the whole system, at everyone. She didn't shower, wore the same sweats for days, watched old sitcoms—Frasier, Modern Family—when she couldn't sleep.

Helene told her parents a sketch of the story because she didn't want the horrible details—the ketchup packet, the pink blanket, the feel and smell of a child dead for two days—to be playing like a movie in anyone else's imagination. Her parents tried to understand, but she felt far away from them. At first, she felt like a girl in a fairy tale who'd blundered off the path and into the woods; she couldn't find her way back. Later, she would realize there could never have been a happy ending; she wasn't the little girl. The hero. She was the villain in disguise. She needed to turn herself into something else or she wouldn't survive. She couldn't go to Kimmey Street, couldn't drive to Georgetown, couldn't get anywhere near the courthouse.

A few weeks later, she'd run through her savings. Helene caught a glimpse of herself in the bathroom mirror. *You're not dead*, she thought; then she brushed her teeth for the first time in days and showered.

Helene got a job waitressing at a restaurant in one of the nice hotels near the beach. The job seemed safe enough, she'd waitressed some in college and remembered how fast the shifts would go. It would be a way to get through the days. She'd do it for the summer, she told herself. Then see what came up.

And the job did help. She found she liked the summer crowd— everyone transient, no one asking any more of her than the food and the check. She loved working near the ocean. She'd come to work early, leave her shoes in the car, and walk the beach barefoot. She could never get all the sand off, but she learned to like the feel of it, a reminder of the calm moments, the soothing hush of the breakers. Helene learned to keep herself in the day by focusing only on what she was doing, listening while she took the orders, looking at the place settings on the tables, cleaning and organizing the wait station when there was a lull. She found she was great at her job, and so grateful for it. "You are here," she told herself, and she'd root herself into her day.

Later, after her shift, she'd go out drinking with the people she worked with, wake up at noon and do it all again. She got used to the rhythm, to the way her life had rearranged itself. She got used to the quiet, sunlit days, and the nights filled with company, laughter and talk while they carried trays, complained about customers. It was an enormous relief. No emergency phone calls, no visits, no days that ended with her sitting in the parking lot, her head on the steering wheel. At the end of the day, her body felt tired, but not her soul.

She waitressed through the summer and then the fall, and when Christmas came that first year, she made a New Year's resolution that she'd find a different job. Dutifully, she looked at the want ads, but every time she'd thought about going back to something like social work, she felt nothing but sadness, even despair. She decided, finally, that she was happy right where she was.

When careers came up in conversation she'd say, "I used to be a social worker, but this pays better and hurts less," or "I'm better at feeding people than judging them." It was true, and it made people laugh and almost no one asked more questions after that.

MORNINGS SHE SPENT READING in bed, weird stuff—1940s detective novels or the biographies of scientists and inventors, no romances, nothing that centered on families or kids. Sometimes she missed talking about the books, missed the discussions she and Peter used to have, but she loved her solitary mornings, her quiet apartment, coffee with too much cream. In November, the wind howling around the corner of the building while she hid under the covers, reading. Sometimes she'd date someone, but she never let anything get serious.

Three years passed. Peter still called every couple of months. His messages were always the same. "It's me again. I just want to know you're okay. I won't give up, so you really should just answer one of these days."

When she finally did answer, Peter didn't miss a beat, sounded as natural as if they'd spoken yesterday, though Helene's pulse pounded in her wrists and neck. Before they hung up, Peter said, "Please have lunch with me. Okay? That's all. Just lunch."

She surprised herself by saying yes. "But," she said, "I don't want to talk about it. You know what I mean. I just can't talk about it, so as long as you're okay with that, then yes. I guess. Yes."

"DAPHNE," HE'D CALLED HER at that first lunch, after all the small talk, after she'd caught him up on her life, as he downed the last of his wine. "You turned yourself into something different, something safe."

Helene watched him put on his serious, fatherly face, the one he used to deliver verdicts, and she burst out laughing. "I didn't turn myself into a laurel tree. I'm not mythological. You only get to judge me if I come before your court. Jesus, were you always this egotistical?"

Then he laughed too. "Yes, but you were too young to notice. Besides," he said, "there's nothing wrong with safe. It's underrated really."

"I think it's more like stable," she said, "and happy. I'm happy."

Peter smiled and motioned to the waitress for another drink. "I'm glad," he said, "I like this new you. But, I just want to say, too, that you were good at what you did. If you ever want to come back—"

"I won't."

After that, they were friends. Kind of friends. Peter always was the one to call her, and she walked away from every lunch, every coffee, thinking it was the last, surprised herself a little every time she said yes again. Though they never stretched for conversation, Helene always worried as she drove to meet him. She'd think that they really had nothing left to say to each other. They lived in two different worlds.

A couple of times the Tyler case rose into their talk like a ghost ship on a gray ocean, but Helene shut it down. "I never understood," Peter said once, "why you took it so hard. Why you couldn't turn and face it and forgive yourself."

"It's over," she'd said then. "I did what I did."

BUT IT WASN'T OVER. That's what she knew as she fast-walked through the dark parking garage to the hospital. Peter, her parents, friends, they all pitied her, saw her self-torment as a kind of collateral damage to a terrible situation that could never have been anything else. She knew the truth, though, the detail they didn't have, and now she knew that she would never feel right, feel whole, until she told the story, and told it to Peter. Only he could understand what she'd done, bring it into the light. She wondered suddenly if maybe he'd always known that. Maybe that was why he kept giving her the chance, a chance to knit what happened into the pattern of her life.

Helene had been scheduled to meet with Sandra Tyler three days before the day she'd come over and found April dead. It was Sandra who'd asked to reschedule the meeting; she'd told Helene she had a date with her ex-husband, that things were looking up. They'd chatted on the phone for almost half an hour while Helene drove down Route 13 to meet another client. Late spring, the fields wore a veil of green, and lilac bloomed at their edges. Helene pictured Sandra in her kitchen, could hear the sound of cartoons and Jesse's voice in the background. That was how their conversations had been ever since the first meeting at the halfway house. Helene had come to think of Sandra as something between a client and a friend, though everything in her training had warned her against that.

Right before they got off the phone, Helene asked, "Where are you going for the date?"

Sandra hesitated.

And in that moment, Helene knew the date was a lie. She knew it.

The light in front of her turned red, and she slowed to a stop. She looked down at her own hands on the steering wheel as she tightened and loosened her grip. Helene tried to find the words to call Sandra on the lie, but everything she could think of made her sound to herself like a bitch, like one of the hard-eyed women she worked with.

When the light changed, Helene eased into the intersection. She thought, *Why should Sandra have to tell me where she's going?* She pictured herself in her parents' kitchen telling them that she was going away for the weekend with a girlfriend. She wondered what lies Peter told his wife. She thought, *Maybe Sandra's seeing another guy.* Maybe that's it. The even lines of corn and soy ticked against her peripheral vision as she drove. Sandra was talking fast now, too brightly, and it made Helene go still inside.

She thought back over her last meeting with Sandra; there'd been no signs of drug use, no change in the house, in her color or health, no red flags. Helene noticed a hawk perch on a wire. Sandra was explaining, a spill of words, giving her too much detail. All the things she and her husband had said to each other about the date, all the specifics. Helene wanted to stop her, tell her that she didn't need to do it. Didn't need to report where she was every moment. Had she surrendered her privacy when she recovered her children?

Helene pulled to the side of the road to think. She put the car in park and leaned her head on the steering wheel. "Sandra," she said, "you sound really good, happy. And you would tell me—right?—if everything weren't okay?"

Sandra laughed, "You'd be the first to know. Honestly! I'm better than ever."

So, Helene made a choice on the side of Route 13 that came out of everything she was, her own understanding of dignity, of privacy, but also her own lies, her illusions. Her own sense that one person could be many people and not all of them sat together comfortably.

Sometimes Helene still woke up in the night hearing Sandra say it. Better than ever.

"Junkies lie." That's what everyone in the office said. "You know how you know a junkie's lying? Her mouth's moving." It used to strike Helene as hypocritical. She'd think, *Oh, you've never lied in your life. Pure as the driven snow.*

Helene had been a liar, a counselor, a daughter, a friend where maybe she shouldn't have, a mistress, a student, a waitress.  She'd been inside and outside of the world she grew up in. But she didn't know then, not at twenty-four, how many people anyone could be. She thought there was a limit. So, she chose for Sandra what she wanted for herself—to be seen as the best of who she was in the moment.

HELENE RECOGNIZED THE VOLUNTEER at the information desk from a few hours earlier. The woman smiled at Helene and took her driver's license, and as she wrote down the information, Helene looked at the veins snaking down the backs of the woman's hands, the age spots, the charm bracelet.

"I'm here to see—"

"Judge Davis, yes," the woman said. She looked at the computer screen. "Oh," she said, smiling, "he's been moved. He's out of ICU."

"He is?" Helene took a full breath.

"Room 324," the volunteer said. "Same elevator as before, but get off one floor earlier."

Helene was already moving; she tossed her thanks back over her shoulder. She squeezed in the elevator beside a doctor with a long blonde braid and an older woman on a stretcher, and she imagined Peter sitting up, maybe even eating, though she knew that was far-fetched. He was out of ICU. She could hardly believe it.

As the elevator rose, her thoughts lightened. She imagined having him over to dinner, introducing him to her parents. She thought of all the ways that she'd done just what he'd said: she'd run away from everything, run away from the girl she'd been, turned herself for better or worse into who she was now. She wanted to explain, tell him that she was sorry for blocking him out, to tell him the story. She saw now that her life was almost whole, that the girl she'd been then could sit beside the woman she was now. But only if she could turn and face it all, face herself, all her selves—even the arrogant, well-meaning, lying girl.

The elevator door slid open to a quiet chaos of moving machines and somber nurses. She looked down the tiled hallway, saw a man who looked so much like a younger Peter that she gasped, and almost called his name out loud. The man stood just outside the door of a room talking quietly into his phone.

P. J. She suddenly realized it was his son.

She saw the faces of everyone around him and understood suddenly what was happening. Peter was out of ICU not because he would live, but so he could die. Helene felt her stomach clench. She wouldn't see Peter again. But she needed to, she just wanted to see his face.

When his son stepped back in the room, Helene moved toward the door. But her feet froze. She imagined Kat looking up at her, imagined herself trying to explain. She circled around the nurses' station and stood on the other side of the hall, looking across. She couldn't see Peter's face at all, just the end of the bed, the contour of his feet.

P. J. leaned against the window beside a woman who must have been his wife, the darkness behind them pierced by a flashing red light. P. J. smiled thinly as he talked to someone Helene couldn't see, someone she imagined was Kat, sitting near the head of the bed. Helene pictured Kat holding Peter's hand, staring into his face. Children sat on the floor, quiet, coloring in books. *Grandchildren*, she thought, *there they are.*

Two younger men arrived, and P. J. wrapped them in an embrace. Helene wondered who they were. She wondered if more people would arrive. She imagined herself in Peter's place, imagined a room filled with all the people she had known and loved in her life. A woman walked down the hall toward her, and she had the strangest thought that it might be another of Peter's lovers—had he had more?—come to stand beside her and watch.

Helene almost laughed. She thought then that she hadn't known Peter well, hadn't tried to, and she wished she had. The man she knew—the judge, the unfaithful husband, the faithful friend—was a sliver of the selves he'd been.

Memories flooded her. A rainy afternoon in bed with Peter, when they'd laughed together about the word "jurisprudence." She understood what she hadn't before—that she was not a point on a line going forward, always shedding the old, but a gathering, a distillate of everyone she'd ever been, and maybe everyone she could ever be.

Who would Jesse Tyler be now at twenty-four, the same age she was when he'd held his dead sister's hand and said, "She's a good baby." Who were those children sitting on the floor and how would this moment change who they became?

A nurse touched her on the shoulder. "Can I help you find someone?"

# SYMPATHY

When she came back to work after Jeff died, the kids presented her with the cards they'd made, walking up to her desk and putting their contribution on the pile, saying, as they'd been instructed, "I'm sorry, Mrs. Donahue."

The construction paper cards—sapphire, vermillion, emerald—looked nothing like the Hallmark sympathy selection, all pastels and soothing script and seashells. Anita, the principal, had visited the class to tell them the news, to explain.

She told Sylvie later that Marla asked, "Will she still be a missus?" That Joe said, "What do you draw? Like a tombstone or something? Like Halloween?"

Anita told them to draw the things that would make them a little happier if they were sad. So the cards rioted with pictures of dogs and cats, candy bars, Pokémon, Mickey Mouse ears, bicycles, skateboards, footballs, butterflies, a bowl of oatmeal, a pair of red basketball sneakers with a Nike swoosh on the side.

Months later, snowed in for four days, Sylvie tried to shovel the walk herself and got only halfway before her feet ached with cold and her shoulders screamed. Bowtie ran around the yard chasing something she couldn't see, his fur frosted with snow, exuberant, running back to her, barking and then darting away. She looked out over the white expanse around her. It was all too heavy to lift.

# BACK

"The sex addiction was worse than the drugs," she said. "Way worse. And it isn't like you can just quit it forever like drugs. Right? It's like a food addiction that way. You gotta eat. You gotta fuck."

Doug looked down the beach at the bent backs and muffled heads to make sure none of his students or colleagues were close enough to hear what she said, what she might say, which, he thought, was any damn thing at all. He thought of excusing himself, thought of pulling out his cell phone and making up a call, but instead he leaned his weight down on the long pole, working it into the frozen sand. They were planting beach grass. The University of Delaware did this every year one Saturday in March, a big volunteer project—undergraduates from his program, graduate students from the College of Marine Studies, or whatever they called it now—alumni, professors, students, staff.

Doug looked forward to it, seeing former students, seeing his current students out of the classroom, everyone laughing, working together for a good cause. Years ago, back when he'd taught Marlie, he'd been the cool new professor, in his thirties; now he felt more like the grand old man, sixty in June.

"Am I embarrassing you?" Marlie asked. She ran a hand through her short brown hair that the wind kept lifting in tufts, showing the gray at the roots. "I mean, you're a psychology professor. This can't be the first time you've ever talked about cross addiction, sex addiction, all that shit."

"Of course you are not embarrassing me," Doug said, but he heard the stiffness in his voice, the "are not" coming out all formal and "maiden aunt," and he didn't look at her. Instead, he bent and untangled two delicate brown stalks from the bunch, set them down deep, tamped the sand around them.

He thought of his wife and their two-year-old grandson at home. They'd been curled up under the fleece blanket watching cartoons when he left. He'd been glad to get away from the insipid music and the noisy chaos of the boy. Now he wished himself back.

He and Christine had had a big fight two weeks ago, a fight about their daughter. Julia. Her name swam into his head and stopped his thoughts. She was divorcing the bartender—her third husband. Christine and Doug had only barely gotten to know him, but he seemed like a kind man, seemed good with Cullen. Now she worked two part-time jobs, and she did what she'd done in the past: gather alimony and child support until the next marriage. He thought of her last visit. Nothing seemed to please her. Nothing he or Christine did or said. Not her favorite lasagna, the flowers Christine put in her room, the train set for the boy. It was all wrong. A disorganized and moody mother, a woman who wore her unhappiness like a brittle candy shell, all sweetness until you broke through—she wanted to move back home, move back in with their grandson. For Cullen, that's what she said. Just temporarily, just for now.

Doug believed they should let her do it. "If that's what she needs," he had said.

Christine shook her head, "She's our only daughter." He thought of seeing Cullen when he came home from teaching classes, the joy of having the boy in the house, his laughter at meals, taking him to the park.

And Julia, too, maybe they could help fix whatever had gone wrong. He knew it would be hard, losing the privacy, losing the quiet. And living with Julia again, as she was now, that awful fake smile, her bitterness like a perfume that seemed, even after she left, to pervade the house. He felt torn.

Christine, though, was definite. She said allowing Julia to move back would be a terrible mistake. "Back," she said, "That's exactly what it would be! It sends the wrong message. We are telling her she's weak. We are telling her she's incompetent. We can help her get a place near here. We can watch Cullen, give her money, but we've got to tell her to find her own way, find her life."

He told her she was heartless.

She told him he was enabling. An icy silence fell, and then the screaming.

They found long nails to open old wounds.

Christine brought up all the times in graduate school when he'd been too busy to play with his daughter, to eat dinner with them, to put Julia to bed. He reminded Christine of the trip to Paris she'd wanted so much, the grant she'd gotten to study there, the months they'd left Julia with Christine's mother.

The fight escalated and escalated. They stalked each other all over the house, shouting and crying.

When the worst of it had passed, they'd collapsed at the foot of their bed, legs stretched out. The sun had gone down, the lights still out. They each talked about their own failures, their own guilt.

Had they been bad parents? They had not been perfect.

But what did it mean to be a good parent to Julia now?

They'd agreed finally, quietly, there in the dark. Julia couldn't move back, but they could help her get her own place. He thought Christine was probably right. He'd always been the softer one, the one to bend the rules, to give in to more ice cream or ten more minutes before bedtime. Maybe that had hurt Julia more than he knew.

"What if she really needs to come home?" he had said. "What if we're wrong?"

Christine reached for his hand, threaded her fingers through his. "We can change our minds if we need to. I just think we have to give her a chance to see what she can do on her own."

After that night, Doug felt like they'd emerged from some thorny woods and were standing in a clearing, on new ground. He felt closer to Christine now, knew that they both felt it, this deepening of love over time, through conflict. He wished he could go back home and sit beside Christine under the blanket with Cullen on his lap eating blueberries. He wished he could be anywhere but standing across from Marlie on this cold beach. It occurred to him that Marlie was about the same age as Julia. He looked at the girl again.

Though, she wasn't a girl. Neither was Julia, as Christine had pointed out patiently over and over. He could see Marlie's age as he looked at her, framed against the sky—the crepe skin at her neck, the exclamation point between her eyes.

The March wind whipped up whitecaps as far out as the horizon behind her and scoured sand into their faces and through their hair. Marlie seemed to lift her chin into it, but Doug finally dropped his eyes, lowered his head, heard the distinctive booming laugh of one of the boys in his Psych 403 class well over to the left. Doug tried to formulate a question to ask Marlie that might tell him something real, something about Julia maybe, about any of them, anyone her age, but the one in his head—*why is everyone your age so fucked up?*—that one he couldn't ask.

"What's up with the rest of your class?" he said instead. "Do you keep in touch with anyone?"

Marlie didn't know anyone anymore, that's what she said. No one from her class, no one at all, really. She didn't have any friends. She'd seen the announcement about the Beach Grass Planting in the paper. "I'm trying," she said, "to reconnect with myself, with a younger, better version of me. Do you remember what I was like back then? When I was your student? How happy I was?"

When Doug had first seen her standing alone on the beach, just beyond the rest of the group, he thought she was younger, someone's little sister. He hadn't recognized her at all. Her hair, which in her twenties she'd worn in long messy brown curls and often dyed pink or purple at the tips, had been shorn off, a boy's cut around her ears. In college, she'd been curvy, now she looked thin, frail, wearing jeans that sagged at the ass and a jacket too light for the blustery cold. She'd walked right over to him and said, "Hello, Doug! Or do I still have to call you Dr. Phillips."

"Marlie? Is it?"

"It's Marlie."

The challenge in her eyes, her obvious plan to commandeer his time and attention, made him want to run.

Marlie plunged her stick into the sand. "I was so happy. Remember? Just bopping around. I assumed it would all go so well."

Doug pictured not Marlie, but Julia at eighteen, remembered the summer just before she'd started college. She'd been a lifeguard at the community pool. He'd packed her lunch in the mornings—peanut butter and marshmallow fluff. He remembered her bounding down the stairs before she left for work or a date, her brown hair streaked blonde, her face tanned and smiling. How full of hope she'd been. He remembered standing at the front door one evening, watching Julia leave for dinner with friends. Christine had been trimming the front flowerbed; Julia had kissed Christine on the top of her head as she'd skipped by.

"I'll be home late!" Julia called.

"You look beautiful," Christine called back. And Julia had looked beautiful, so much life, blooming like one of the roses Christine tended.

They both watched the car pull away. "We did good," Christine said, and he'd believed it.

"I do remember you," he said to Marlie. And he did. He remembered her too tight clothes, the kind of desperate sexuality that felt, even then, dangerous. He remembered the spring day she'd come into his class wearing a half-top and hot pants, although he supposed they didn't call them that anymore. She'd worn a silver chain around her waist that dipped down and hung just under her belly button, and he'd watch the boys watch her as she'd crossed in front of the room to take her seat. He supposed some of that had been for him, maybe that's why she was here again. He pushed the thought away.

"I remember meeting your parents at graduation," he said. "You were happy . . . full of hope." He pictured himself standing in the broiling sun wearing the black robes over the gray suit, sweating so hard that his socks and underwear were soaked. Her parents blurred in his memory into all the parents at all the graduations, flowered dresses and handshakes and the joy and boredom of all graduation days. He tried to remember Julia's graduation, but he couldn't. He searched his memory again. How could he have forgotten? Filed it with the others? He remembered bits of the party afterward. They'd rented a room in a restaurant. It had been raining. What was the name of that place? He remembered an upstairs room, brick and dark wood, standing near a window and watching the streaks of rain down the window like tears down a face, suddenly shining in the lights of passing cars.

"Are you living in the area again?" he asked Marlie.

Yes, of course she was. Living with her mom and dad, getting her life together. Doug nodded, and the argument with Christine slammed into him. That's what parents do, he thought. He wanted to take her to Christine, to say, "See! We're doing the wrong thing."

Marlie squatted low, holding the pole as if she were sighting along a rifle barrel. "I wish I could go back," she said, staring down the beach at the students. They laughed and shouted to one another, some took pictures to post online, making a human pyramid, holding bunches of beach grass up behind their heads.

"It's never as easy as it seems on the outside though." Doug's eye found Jasmine Ramirez, whose mother had died of cancer just months ago. "You can't . . . you know what all the counselors say, don't compare your insides and other people's outsides . . ." He trailed off. Marlie sat in the sand, started talking again, describing her room at the rehab. The monastic cell with the single bed and the wooden cross on the wall—a Christian place. The single white washcloth and scratchy towel to take to the community shower, her soap and shampoo in a bucket. She started fucking one of the women on her floor, started doing it in the shower. They'd gotten caught. The Christians kicked her out. What did he think about that?

He looked up at her over his shoulder as he patted the sand around another stalk of grass. Her eyes strained toward something that might appear on the horizon at any moment, land, maybe, or a ship. Doug thought of the history of the towns along the Delaware coast—fishing villages where people looked out to sea just like Marlie was now, longing, grieving something or someone who would never come back.

"You're there because you're an addict," she said, "and then they kick you out because you're cross-addicted. You're a psychologist. What's the deal with that?"

"I'm a psychology *professor*," Doug said. "That's a big difference."

"Right, those who can do, and all that," she said, walking over to where the bundles of beach grass lay.

Doug felt a flash of heat through his chest that beat in his wrists and hands. He gripped the pole hard and jammed it into the sand. "Maybe," he called, trying to bite back the "fuck you." "Maybe it isn't someone else's fault they kicked you out. Maybe you got kicked out because you didn't think the rules applied to you. You think you're special. Maybe if you took responsibility for your own life, you wouldn't be so unhappy." It all came out in a rush, getting more and more vehement. The force of it stunned him, like he was watching some other Doug say it.

But she only smirked at him, satisfied, he thought, to have gotten the reaction, her eyes hard and bright. And he was angrier than before. Angry at himself for taking the bait, at her for ruining his morning, at the cold wind in his face. At Julia. He looked down the beach a couple of hundred feet at the group of students he wished he were standing with—Jasmine Ramirez, Dustin Purcell, Janey Passwaters. Good kids, nice kids, laughing together. Not drug addicts, sex addicts. Though what did you know, what did you *ever* know about anyone?

Was Julia addicted? Would he know if she was?

"Thanks, Dad," Marlie said, "for the good advice. I'll certainly take it under consideration. All my fault, is it, Dad? Your old refrain. So good to have this conversation with you again."

He thought he must have misheard her. He shook his head hard, trying to dislodge the word. "Dad?" he said. He felt suddenly disoriented, like the world had lurched on its axis.

Marlie smirked harder at him. Sat down on the sand cross-legged, looking at him as though from a great distance or from behind a one-way mirror the way they used to watch groups interact in grad school. He wanted to walk over and shake her, but he felt hollowed out. "I'm not your father. I'm . . ."

Could Julia be addicted? Quickly, desperately, he checked down the list he'd memorized years ago for some exam—changes in mood or behavior, changes in weight, lethargy, loss of enthusiasm for former interests, red eyes, bruising.

He tried to remember her eyes, her arms. Couldn't the divorces explain all of it? Being a single mom? Couldn't that explain the bitterness and exhaustion? But what had caused the divorces then?

"You might as well be my father," Marlie said. "You're so like him. Why is it every old dude I know has this 'pull yourself up by your own bootstraps' world view? So goddamn predictable. Do you think it's an expression of your incredible privilege or are you just that scared?"

A gull cut across the blue above him, and Doug suddenly felt the day sheer away like it had been sliced with a knife. The anger rose in his throat again, but with it a kind of sadness he hadn't felt in a long time, maybe since his own father died.

"And how is it that grownups—'adult children,' that's the term—children who've been given everything, every advantage, every privilege, can fuck up their lives to the point that they run back to mommy and daddy, to their house and their money, and yet feel so perfectly free to criticize them? Maybe your dad has more faith in you than you have in yourself. Maybe what he's trying to do is tell you to find your own way, your own life." Christine's words. He could hear her voice as he said them.

For just a moment, looking in Marlie's face, he saw those words land, and he saw, at the same moment, the girl she'd been at twenty, the desperation, the desire to please, the pain just barely masked by bravado. Then Marlie's face stiffened into a mask, and she straightened up and walked away from him without a word, walked to the tideline. Doug watched her stand at the edge, hands shoved in her jeans pockets, toeing shells or rocks out of the wet sand. He thought he should go to her, maybe, maybe apologize. The angry part of him felt vindicated, but mostly he felt something he couldn't quite name. A heaviness in his legs and back, a tightness in his chest when he took a breath. He pressed the stick into the ground again as far as he could. He watched the grains of sand roll back down into the hole.

He looked down to the edge of the water at Marlie, then turned and headed for the small knot of students from his class. They'd planted several long lines of grass along the storm fence by the path back to the parking lot. As he got closer, he could hear their laughter burst through their easy talk.

Jasmine Ramirez straightened up and pointed at him, a stalk of beach grass still in her hand, her black hair beneath her white hat twisting and tangling in the wind. "I've got a question for you, Dr. Phillips," she said. "We've been having a debate about gender identity and—"

She stopped speaking abruptly, her smile disappearing, her eyes opening wide. Doug followed her eyes over his shoulder.

"That girl you were talking to . . ." Jasmine began.

Doug saw it then. Marlie's head under a wave and then above the water and then under again. The heaviness in his body suddenly felt immense, leaden. "Oh," he said, "Oh, Jesus Christ. She's gone in."

Someone screamed off to his right. Doug felt himself moving, but the air around him thickened. He peeled off his coat and started to run, called back over his shoulder toward Jasmine, toward Dustin, "Stay there. Stay there. Call 911."

He sank in the sand as he ran, threw himself down at the tideline and yanked off his boots, the freezing water drenching his socks, the bottoms of his pants as he pushed himself forward, trying to move, the shock of the cold stopping his breath.

When Julia was four, a wave had washed her under. He and Christine had been holding her hands on either side, not even knee deep, but a rogue wave, like two irresistible arms, had swept her out from between them. Doug remembered the white flash of panic, remembered trying to run against the tide, screaming "No! No!" into the ocean, the sky. Then he'd suddenly seen the bottom of her foot rise almost to the surface, a pale shape, and he'd grabbed her ankle and pulled her up, crying. Frightened, but fine. He'd lifted her into his arms, her head against his chest, her cold wet hair plastered to her face.

"Why are you doing this?" he shouted. To Marlie, to himself, to Julia.

As he got deeper in, Doug had to push himself up over the waves that crashed in his face, blurred his vision. The whole world was gray and cold. He licked the salt from his lips. Where was she? He tried swimming a few strokes, but his clothes were weights, dragging him deeper, tugging left and right. He looked for the shape of her head, couldn't see it. He felt the cold like a band around his chest, constricting his breath. The next roller pulled him under, and he pushed himself up, surfaced again. He swallowed a mouthful of cold salt water and rose above the crest of the next wave, choking.

The waves broke over him again and again. He opened his mouth to the air.

And then something broke inside of him. Broke like a wave—cold, salt, certain. He remembered Julia's face as she'd left after dropping off Cullen, saw her again pulling out of their driveway, waving at them through the windshield, light and shade playing over it like water.

He knew it then. Maybe he'd known it all along. The word settled at the bottom of his mouth, under his tongue, a stone, gray and heavy. Addict. He felt the weight of it.

Addict.

Addict.

The dread of saying it out loud, to Christine, to Julia, to anyone. A cold gray equation. Julia is. Julia is.

Then Marlie was in front of him. He leapt the next wave and stretched himself up. Not as deep as he thought, just an inch or so over his head. He bobbed high and took a full breath.

Marlie threw herself under the water when she saw him, wailing, weeping, trying to move away, out deeper and deeper, flailing against the current. But he got close enough to grab the sleeve of her jacket and he tugged until her hand came to the surface, pale and almost lifeless. He pulled her toward him, lifted her, her arm around his neck, head against his chest.

"I'm sorry," she sobbed. "I'm sorry. I'm sorry."

She was taller than he expected, but light, feather light, and he cradled her as the water pushed them in toward the shallows, hissing as they retreated. Her blue lips parted, tried to make words. A deep shivering shook her frame.

He was knee deep when he saw the red and blue flashing lights in the parking lot, the paramedics running toward them, running down the freshly planted dunes, dragging the stretcher over the new grass to the edge of the water.

"Everything's going to be alright now," he soothed. "Everything. You'll see. We'll get you back. We'll get you back."

# DO SOMETHING

When the call came, I half knew it would be her. I'd been on two other suicide attempt calls in the last three months and they were both the same woman. She was forty; her name was Marlie. So when dispatch said "Exposure and possible suicide attempt," I figured there was a good chance.

The last time we saw Marlie, I was working with Johnny. He's new, but not as new as me, and he's a paramedic, so he's got more school. He's got a year in the field; I've got six months next week.

I was in nursery school when the planes hit the towers in 2001. I'm twenty-one years old this year. I feel like I remember that day, but I don't; I have everyone else's memories. Jackie, my sister, moved to New York to be a firefighter, to be part of the rebuilding. That's what she said. God, I loved her. She was exactly seven years older than me, and since I was born on her birthday, Mom and Dad let her name me. Her favorite movie when she was seven was *Cars*, so she named me after the Porsche that Lightning McQueen falls in love with, Sally after Sally Carrara. I guess it's kind of dumb, being named after a car, but I like my name, like that Jackie gave it to me.

I have Jackie's picture with me, either in my wallet or in the locket my mom gave me after Jackie died. I don't like jewelry, just that necklace I wear all the time. At work, I don't usually think about anything except the call we're on, the moment. That's one of the great things about work. I just move. All day—if we aren't on a call, I'm cleaning the rig or the station, doing inventory, whatever. Just keep moving. I think better when I move, feel better. But sometimes afterwards, when I'm trying to get to sleep, I touch the locket and talk to Jackie. She was killed on I-95 in Jersey when the driver in the car in front of her stopped because he was having a stroke. My sister got out to help. Another car hit her.

Dad encouraged me when I said I wanted to be an EMT, but Mom cried. "Can't I have one kid who wants to be something safe? An accountant or a teacher or something?" She said, "You don't have to do this for her, you know. She wouldn't want you to do this for her."

But I'm not an EMT for Jackie. It's been my dream as long as I can remember. In first grade, we wrote thank you notes to all the first responders. In fifth grade, we had a poster on the classroom wall of three firefighters that said, "There When You Need Us."

JOHNNY AND I LOADED UP the beach stretcher, hit the siren, raced down Route 1. Route 1 in March looks like a ghost town—strip malls with every other store open, grey snow piled in the median. I like the summer with all the action, the people, but there's something about the beach in March, the clean, gray, quiet. I was driving; Johnny was on the computer. "Not much info on this one," he said.

"What do you want to bet it's Marlie again?" I said. "I'll bet you Starbucks it is."

Johnny shook his head. "Nah," he said. "No way. Open water? Middle of the day? Not her style."

"Mochaccino!" I said, as soon as we made it over the dunes. It was her again alright. I could tell even as I watched the guy who was carrying her, watched him trudging through the soft sand. It was her hair, her size. Her body. Funny the way you get to know people's bodies in this job. One of the things that's surprised me these last few months is how many things happen in bathrooms, in bedrooms, how often we're slicing through clothes, and then just all the smells—the puke and piss and sweat. You can see the whole story of a person's life written right on them, the stretch marks from the kids they had forty years ago, the scars from the heart bypass. The coke addict with the flat nose; the bulimic with the brown, terrible teeth. Bodies are like books, or ledgers maybe.

Me, I'm almost five feet tall, if I take a deep breath. I'm skinny, like Jackie was. I can wear kid's clothes. Because of my size, everyone thinks that I'm girly or frail. Another thing that's great about this job is that I surprise people all the time with how strong I am, how much I can lift. I can help you get a wet 400-pound drunk out of a bathtub. I can climb anything—trees, trellises. When I first started working here, some of the guys called me "Squirt" and talked around me when something big was going down. They don't do that anymore.

Johnny was wrong, but he was right, too. This attempt was weird, not her style. The first time we found her drunk in the ladies' room at Irish Eyes, a bar that looks out over the canal in Lewes. During the day, the fishing boats dock there, and at night the lights slide across the water. Marlie hadn't really meant to die. All show. She was crouched in the corner with a switchblade, and she'd cut herself up, but she hadn't sliced deep except in one place near her elbow, and even there, she hadn't gotten an artery or anything. They stitched up her arms and her chest in ER; most of the gashes wouldn't even scar.

I cut my eyes over to Johnny running beside me, his hand guiding the stretcher, the big, gray wheels kicking up sand, but he didn't look back at me. Instead, he said it out loud,

"Miss Marlie." There was something in his voice, a kind of gentleness, like he was sad that she'd done it again.

The second time, when Marlie tried to OD, Johnny had been the same way. He had sympathy. Her mother met us at the door, wrung like a dishrag and crying. We maneuvered the stretcher up the curved staircase to the white and gold bathroom. It was one of those mansions in Harbor Cove, a development that had security gates and fake ponds at the entrance. The whole place had been cornfields when I was a kid and now it was all houses. I wondered how it happened. How people ended up coming to live here. I wondered about all the lives in the houses, all the bodies, the stories.

When we got to the bathroom, her father was lifting her out of the tub and wrapping her in a red beach towel. He was a small man, but wiry and tough.  He sat her on the edge of the stretcher like she was a little girl, and he tried over and over to keep the towel from falling. I guess he was embarrassed for her, but she didn't seem to care. She shivered even though the bathroom was steaming hot, even though she was sweating, too, and bright red.

Johnny put his hand under her chin and shined a light in her eyes and asked her what state she lived in. Delaware. He asked her what she'd taken, and she said twenty Tylenol PMs. Responsive.

"I just wanted to sleep," she said.

"That's not a great way to do it," Johnny said. "When did you take the medicine?" His tone was even, calm. He held her hand while he spoke to her, taking her pulse. He listened to her heart. I saw the empty Tylenol bottle over behind the toilet and held it up.

"Did you take anything else with it?" he asked. "Drink anything?"

"A shot for courage," she said softly, a little smile.

I didn't get it. What in the world could make a forty-year-old woman do something like take twenty Tylenol?

I mean, you've made it that long, what can be so bad? But then, she didn't seem to have much, not for being as old as she was. No husband, no kids, living with her parents, no job, probably no insurance. Sometimes when I picture my future, I scare myself that I'll end up like this. Failure to launch or whatever. Since Jackie died, I just have more trouble seeing a future for myself. Maybe it's because, growing up, Jackie did something and then I did it—braces, boyfriends, driver's licenses. She did everything first. Even dying.

I tried to talk to Mom about it. I was home on a Saturday afternoon because I was working the night shift. She was sitting at the kitchen table with spreadsheets piled around the computer and in sliding stacks on the floor. End-of-quarter and tax time, she runs the financial office for a logistics company, so it was a bad time to try to talk.

Right after Jackie died, my mom stopped dying her hair. It bothered me. Not that she looks bad, her hair is a strong iron gray: a salt and pepper mix. But she looks older, or she looks closer to her real age, fifty-one.

That's how our conversation about moving out started. I didn't plan on getting so serious. I just asked her about dying her hair, if she would ever start doing that again. I guess what I was asking is if we'd ever go back to the way things used to be, like we were before the accident.

My mom stopped typing and reached up to touch her hair. Then she smiled. "It doesn't seem that important these days," she said. "Besides, I'm going to be sixty."

"In nine years!" I cracked open a Coke, and she tsked at me.

"You'll be healthier when you're sixty if you stop drinking that sugary crap." My mom was a gymnast growing up. She runs and lifts weights and eats the cleanest of anyone I know.

I laughed, "You'll still be telling me that when I'm sixty."

"Oh, no, my girl! I'll be long gone. You'll have to fend for yourself then. You'll be telling your own kids not to drink Coke."

*My own kids.* It sounded impossible. I hadn't had a boyfriend since sophomore year of high school, right before Jackie died. I'd gone on dates, but nothing had clicked. I thought sometimes if I moved out it would be easier, but even thinking of it made me feel lonely. Not just for myself, but for my mom and dad, too.

"I don't think I'll ever have kids," I said to my mom.

She closed her computer and looked at me. "You've always wanted kids."

"I don't know." I felt suddenly tired. I took another swig of Coke. "Who knows what will happen in the future?"

"No one," she said, "but that doesn't mean that you can't plan, can't want things." She always did this, like she could see inside my head. Jackie had wanted kids. She used to pick out names for them that I made fun of, like Isadore and Silas. "Your father and me—we'll be fine. And so will you. Life will go on, I promise."

I wonder if Marlie had been afraid to move out, or had moved out and then moved back in because her parents were lonely. We saw that all the time. Older folks living alone who called the EMTs not because they were really sick, but because they were lonely. They wanted someone to listen to them maybe, to see them. Like Mrs. Shipley. We bring her in almost every Friday with chest pain, but she's fine. She lives in another development off the highway, Bayside Harbor. They're all "Harbor" something. Sometimes there's only one or two lights on in the whole neighborhood. Her garden is clean and neat, and in the fall, there are always mums and pumpkins on the porch. She has a grand piano in her living room, and when I asked her if she played, she said that she had studied for years, that she loved music, but that she doesn't play anymore. It made me sad to think of her sitting alone looking at the keys, no one to listen. The house is always immaculate, no dust on the piano, no laundry anywhere. Mrs. Shipley burns candles, and it smells like vanilla or pine when you come through the door. But who comes through the door besides us and the aids?

TELL THEM ANYTHING else you've taken," Marlie's mother said, her eyes darting from Johnny to Marlie. "Tell them everything."

Marlie shook her head.

Johnny turned and looked at me. Not too bad, his eyes said, "Load and go," and I nodded, and we got her sorted onto the stretcher as fast as we could and hoisted her down the stairs.

But then we were losing her en route. I radioed it in. The ER nurse sounded surprised. "Didn't she take Tylenol? Was there something else?"

"Tylenol PM. It's the diphenhydramine," Johnny called. "Her heart rate's dropping."

I hit the gas harder, hit the siren. We made the turn for Route 9, maybe three or four minutes away. I radioed the ER again, "We're incoming, unresponsive." I could hear Johnny in the back shouting at her, "Don't you leave us, Miss Marlie. Stay with me now. Stay with me."

AND HERE SHE WAS. Trying to leave us again.

The cops were just ahead of us on the scene. The guy carrying Marlie had made it through the sand to the edge of the crowd. Another big guy had run down and they were carrying her head and foot.

People sifted down the beach and joined the crowd already forming around us. I couldn't figure out why so many people were there in March. Most of them my age or younger, maybe high school or college. I knew there must have been an event, but I didn't know why there were poles all over the sand, pointed. Some of the kids in the crowd still held the pointed poles, too, and it made me think of Jackie reading me Beauty and the Beast and the illustration of the villagers showing up with pointed sticks and torches to kill the monster, their cartoon faces angry, the dark sky behind them.

Later, when we got back to the station, I found out they were planting beach grass, that people did it every year, a big volunteer event. The beach grass keeps the dunes from eroding, at least for a little while, at least until the next big storm. In the end, of course, nothing works.

As we got closer, I could hear the crowd. A boy called out, "Dr. P. saved her! He went in." Some were holding up cell phones, taking videos. When we got down to the scene, they started closing in, tightening the circle around us. I felt my pulse beating in my arms and hands.

"Give them some air now. Make some space," I said.

I got out the hypothermia tents and shook two hot packs while Johnny stripped Marlie's wet jacket and closed someone's coat tight around her.

Our hypothermia tents are bright blue and green and red, all primary colors. Even when you open them up, they look more like you should use them for a kid's campout in the backyard.

Johnny told me with his eyes to go check on the man who'd carried her in.

"I'm fine," he said, waving me off. He was in his sixties, maybe, and a big guy, shivering in his wet clothes. "I'm fine. Take care of her. Take care of . . . ." The man mumbled something that sounded like "jewels" and took a step backward and his knees collapsed, and he sat down hard just at the line where the beach grass started. He looked up at the sky like he'd never seen it before and then down at his wet socks caked with sand.

His falling sent a shock through the crowd, and they all surged forward at once with a long "oh" sound. I felt the sand shift under my feet. Johnny stood up and grabbed his pack just as I popped open the first tent.

"Get that over him," he said to me, "and then put hot packs under her armpits until you get her in a tent."

"Him first?"

"Right now." Then he crouched next to the man as I pulled the tent over top of us all like an upside-down cup, placed the weights, and shoved in the stakes. Sand sifted down on top of us; our faces bright red, and green and yellow in the colored reflections.

With the tent around us, the wind stopped. Johnny was still taking the man's pulse, which meant it must have been slow or irregular. I heard the man's breathing change.

"We need another rig," Johnny said, and my stomach clenched. I crawled out and told the Sergeant who called it in right away.

When I put my head back in the tent, Johnny said, "Go see how Miss Marlie is. Get her in a tent. Get her hot packs."

Moving the few feet toward her, I felt the sand sting my face, felt the eyes of the crowd, and a loop started in my head, "this is bad, this is bad, this is bad."

"That man had saved her. Dr. P.," the kid said. I tried to picture him in scrubs and a stethoscope. Had I seen him around the hospital?

Suddenly I felt something I never had before. A loose shutter flapping in my chest. That man. This is bad. This is bad. I didn't have enough breath.

I knelt beside Marlie and tried to lift her arm and tuck a hot pack along her body, but she grabbed it away from me and tossed it to the edge of the crowd.

"Miss Marlie. Please let me help you. I'm just trying to get you warm." I said it the way I thought Jackie would have, or Johnny—calm and kind. But I didn't feel that way. I felt furious.

Marlie rolled back and forth in the sand, rolled from her stomach to her back. She wouldn't let me lift her arms or touch her either. She wrapped herself tighter and tighter in the coat. Like maybe she knew what I felt—that she should die if she wanted to, that I should be back there helping to save the man who saved her.

Three times, I thought. Three times she'd tried to die, and we'd come running and everyone tries and cries and then she does it again.

The cop squatted by Marlie's head and said something I couldn't hear.

"Fuck you," Marlie spat at him, and curled herself into a ball.

The hot pack had warmed my freezing hands enough that I finally got the tab on the tent to slide. I got it up over the two of us, but before I could stake it down, the wind grabbed it. I clutched at the strings, the sides, and the fucking wind just laughed at me, lifted it just over my head.

"Jesus," someone screamed as the loose tent grazed the crowd. I couldn't think what to do. The cops, some of the kids, tried to chase the tent down. I watched people scatter in front of me, but it was like a scene in a movie. A new loop started in my head, "Do something. Do something. *Do.*" But I couldn't think what. Should I chase the tent? Never leave your patient until other help has come. I could see it in my own handwriting in the notes I'd taken months ago.

Marlie, I squatted down beside her. I felt her skin. She was cold. She needed the tent. I stood again. Took two steps.

Never leave your patient.

She needs the tent.

I watched the group surround it, trying to catch it, to block its escape. It was an animal intent on getting away. A bird. It flew. Every time the hands got close, the thing lifted just above them. Finally, it settled into the breakers and bobbed around, upside down in the cold water.

Tent. I started down toward the water.

Never leave your patient.

Then I heard the mechanical voice of the defibrillator coming from the other tent. "No heartbeat detected," it said. And then, "Clear." I opened my mouth to call out to Johnny, but I had no air. The man who had saved her was having a heart attack. I swayed where I stood. The sand seeped through the holes in my boots. I looked at my feet, my hands.

The world had turned kaleidoscope, all broken pieces of light and color. I tried to move again, to take another step. I couldn't.

I tasted the sand, gritty in my mouth. I heard the traffic out on the highway, a siren in the distance. Voices the wind almost erased. A constant roar like one wave pouring in, a roar that filled every empty space in me.

Never leave your.

The tent. I need.

Never leave

THE NEXT DAY WE GOT WORD at the station that Dr. P.—Dr. Douglas Phillips, that was his name—had died. Marlie, we heard, was fine, released after a couple of hours, after her body temperature came back to normal.

The memorial service was a week from that day on the beach. It rained, and the cold wind blew the rain sideways under umbrellas and into doors. Johnny told me not to go. Told me that it was a bad habit to start, and I'd end up at too many funerals, caring too much. He said, "You're all in, in that moment, but after, you've got to let go. You've got to."

But I went to the funeral. Sitting in the back, I watched the rain on the stained-glass window beside me. I watched the people shake hands and hug and cry. I saw a couple of kids I knew from high school who'd been his students, a girl named Jane who'd sat beside me in Chemistry class. When she looked at me, I nodded, but

I sat by myself. I didn't belong there. I'd said two words to the man. But I'd come to think of him as someone like the fireman on 9/11, like my sister, someone who died saving someone else.

Marlie didn't come.

THEN THE WEEKS TURNED into months, and now to a year. We never heard from Marlie again. Never got another call. I googled her once, though I know that's wrong, and a couple of times, I've driven past her parents' house, either on a call or just by myself, driving around. I can't tell if they even live there anymore. There's no lawn furniture on the porch. Lights go on and off on a timer.

Johnny says I'll burn out quick if I carry it around. I know that's true. Mostly I don't. I just wish I knew the end of the story. I wonder if his dying changed her. I wonder if she's stopped trying to die.

# TAKING CARE

She looks out the sliding glass door of the double wide, but she doesn't see the scraggly shrubs, the fast-food wrappers under them, even the back of the other trailer with the piece of siding missing. She sees Rayla—the reflection of Rayla—sitting on the blue rocking horse that Donny found at the yard sale. Rayla watching cartoons, wearing the pink Cinderella jammies, her red feet cold, her toes wrapped around the wooden pegs, her thin blonde ponytail bouncing with the rocking of the horse.

Donny didn't work this morning like he said; instead, he's somewhere out in the bay, fishing, and when he stops by—if he stops by like he promised—she's hoping he'll have caught something. Then he'll be in a good enough mood that she can ask him for the money.

She should go get Rayla socks, she thinks, but she doesn't move. Rayla's baby doll, yellow hair matted, lies on the ground by the empty flower bed. Beyond the window, the wind lifts the brown and gold leaves and blows them around the grass and into the corners of the tiny, wooden porch. A siren goes by out on the highway—ambulance or firetruck—and fades in the distance.

Donny's her father, but she always called him Donny, even when she was Rayla's age. No one called him anything else ever. "Except maybe 'son-of-a-bitch,'" he'd say. Then he'd laugh.

And he'd give her the money. She knows it, knows he's had it ever since her grandfather died. And he'd be nice as hell about it and say, "Just pay me back whenever you can." But then if she got her nails done or bought a case of beer or got another tattoo, he'd change his tune. He'd start in on her, making snide comments, rolling his eyes, until she paid it all back.

But she could never keep ahead. A dentist bill, a blown radiator, and she'd have to borrow it again. Like now.

She looks down at the latest tattoo on the top of her right foot, a surfboard with a snake curled around it. She'd never been a surfer, but it reminded her of how much she'd loved the beach growing up, and all those afternoons she and Donny spent together when he'd come home from work out of the blue and off they'd go, her digging in the sand and him surf casting.

That was when Donny and her mom had still been married, when the world seemed like a place that didn't change, before all the outlets went in, before all the developments. Her mom told her later that she'd been a "whoopsie" and that it put a strain on the marriage. Rayla had been a whoopsie, too, but Ray didn't stick around long enough to know the baby as anything but a cry and a bottle. She'd named her Rayla so he'd see that the baby was his and that he should take care of them. Even though he'd left, she'd gotten used to the name. She liked it. "My Rayla of Sunshine," or "Raylalalala."

The name had been a passing thought—"a whim," Donny would have called it. That's what he called her tattoos. But like the tattoos, it stuck. "Women and their whims." It was an expression of Donny's and one of the things that had driven him crazy about her mom, drove him crazy about her. "You never think it through," he'd say. "Nothing. Neither of you.

Livin' hand to mouth, minute to minute." Not that he was any better. He'd promise something, but then if the wind changed, or the waves, you just never knew. She hopes he'll show. She hopes he'll give her the loan.

She'd thought about asking her mom for the money, just enough to cover the rent on the trailer, but she figured her mom likely didn't have it either, working part time since her back went out, cleaning houses when she could, and when she couldn't, collecting disability. How could you plan when life was like that? Babies getting sick and backs going out and cars dying, and then the rent is still due and you still have to get to work.

She had a new job in housekeeping at the hospital and it was nights and weekends, and it was hard as hell to get a sitter and expensive. Lately, her mom had been watching Rayla for her when she worked which helped so much. She couldn't lose this job. She wouldn't. She'd tried lots of things, worked at the dry cleaners, waitressed, temp work as a secretary. But she couldn't make anything stick. She liked working at the hospital though. She liked the name "essential personnel," liked that she felt part of something bigger and important. Even if was just cleaning up the waiting room, wiping down the chairs and arranging the magazines so that they looked inviting, maybe it helped someone feel better somehow.

So she had to talk to Donny.

She pulls her robe around her and reties it at her waist. She feels the tightness against her belly and sucks it in, then thinks she should maybe lose some weight. She slides her hand in the terry cloth pocket. Two beer caps and a few Cheerios she'd picked up off the floor after they spilled out of Rayla's bowl.

She moves the bottlecaps over each other and searches around to find the words to use with Donny, some words she'd never said to him before that might make the whole thing different. Might make him see that this new job gave her a real chance, that she'd be able now to get ahead. Even if something happened.

And how could you stop it from happening? Sometimes she'd wake up at night afraid of dying. Who would take care of Rayla?

LIKE THE NIGHT BEFORE, she'd been mopping up the waiting room in the ER. They'd called her down because a drunk guy puked all over—once in the waiting room, then again in one of the bays, the hallway. The smell gagged her as she sprinkled the baking soda. There were only two other patients in the ER, and they'd moved all the way across the room, as far as they could get. The lights of the cars leaving the parking lot slid over the big windows. She'd learned in her orientation that the hospital had started out as a house in town. Two doctors, brothers, had brought sick people to their home to watch them. They'd built the big new building right next to that first house. It was still there; you could see it from some of the upstairs windows. Sometimes, even when she was doing a nasty job like cleaning a drunk's puke, she'd remember the house and think that she was part of a bigger story.

After she'd cleaned up, she'd gone back to the nursing station. A man had come in an hour or two before—almost drowned maybe or had a heart attack—she couldn't figure it out from the bits she'd heard. For a while, as she emptied trash and dusted signs, everyone ran in and out of the curtained slot the man was in, tossing instructions over her head. It was "all hands on deck," that's what Donny would have said.

When she heard the doctor say, "The widow is on her way," she knew the man had died and she suddenly felt her throat tighten up and her eyes itch like she might cry. Then the nurse came and told her that she'd missed a little patch of puke back out in the waiting room. That's what she was doing when the widow walked in.

The double doors in front of the information desk hissed open. She heard the click of heels on the linoleum and looked up. The little boy beside her, who must have been her grandson, held her hand. He had a bag of Goldfish crackers and a truck. In the hand that wasn't holding his, the woman held his juice box.

The crackers, the truck. She stared at the blue truck in the boy's hand and her breath caught in her throat, and her heart cut itself in half.

This woman had gotten the phone call, the worst phone call of her life—she pictured the woman still holding the phone, standing in some fancy living room with crystal and paintings, looking up from the screen out some window at the nice yard. In the next moment, then, knowing everything, every awful thing she would have to face, the woman took the time to find the blue truck, went to the kitchen and found a juice box and snacks. She imagined the woman looking down at the boy—who didn't understand, who couldn't understand, but who would know something bad had happened—and in this worst of all moments the woman thought only of what would make it better for him. A juice box. A truck.

Still holding the mop, she stared across the floor toward the woman. The woman stood by the welcome desk, eyes scanning the waiting room without seeing her or anyone. The little boy said something, and the woman looked down at him, brushed his bangs with her hand.

She wanted more than anything to know this woman, to be her friend.

It made no sense. She knew it made no sense. But she understood that the woman knew what it meant to take care, to plan, to forget for one second whatever it was you felt or wanted and to think instead about someone else. She thought then that taking care was something she had never really done, had never seen. Her parents had done their best, given her what they could. But she knew suddenly—like a light coming on—she knew that what this woman had done for the boy was love, and she believed that this woman might teach her, change her. She didn't know how to care for anyone yet—not herself, not even Rayla—though that was the closest she'd come. But she knew she could learn. That real care was possible.

The nurse came out and took the woman's arm. She'd stood still staring after them, holding the mop, swaying on her feet. She wanted to follow them back but understood that she couldn't, that it was wrong. She didn't know this person at all. The woman had just lost her husband.

But the picture of the woman, the idea of taking care, she couldn't shake it.

NOW SHE TURNS THE WORD "care" over and over in her mind, thumbing it as she thumbed the bottle caps in her robe pocket. She says it out loud to taste it, and Rayla turns her head from the television. This has to change, she thinks, without knowing what this meant.

Beyond the window of the trailer, Donny's car pulls into the drive. She looks through the shadows moving across the windshield to see if he is smiling.

She goes to the rocking horse and scoops Rayla onto her hip. She wants to say something to her, to promise her that she'd do better, be better. But what would the words mean? She thinks of the widow and the boy, the juice box, the truck. She holds Rayla and looks into her sweet eyes.

"Let's get you some socks," she says.

# TIMELINE

I.

The orange bucket chairs in the waiting room—torture. The oversized TV on an endless Entertainment Channel loop—impossible to ignore, impossible to bear. So, Charmel paced the corridors outside the outpatient surgery waiting room. She thought, *At least I'm getting steps*, then thought, *You're a pretty awful person. No mother should think about how many steps she has when her daughter is in surgery.* That's what her daughter, Thea, had said to her in the middle of their last big fight two weeks ago. "You're a pretty awful person." Charmel had burst out laughing because it was such a seventeen-year-old thing to say, the kind of thing she might easily have said to her own mother at that age, and because she knew she could be a pretty awful person though she tried hard not to be.

Lao Tzu came into her mind: "To know the enemy is to dance with your own shadow." That's what her fights with Thea felt like, dancing with herself or some version of herself. Charmel thought of Thea's face before the nurses wheeled her into the operating room, as the anesthesia kicked in, how soft and sweet, how vulnerable. No. Thea wasn't the enemy. Charmel hated that she'd thought it even for a second. But

Thea was stubborn, and she didn't see how fragile things were, how easily life could wrench dreams away.

Would this injury change everything? Charmel turned to pace in the other direction. Stanford wouldn't give Thea the scholarship if she wasn't going to play. She looked at the door to outpatient surgery. So much depended on something out of their control.

Thea dreamed one year into the future. She would go to Stanford and play volleyball. That was it. No amount of reasoning or pushing had convinced Thea to apply to another school or have a back-up plan. Charmel couldn't decide if it was because Thea naively believed that whatever she planned was sure to come true, or if Thea stubbornly refused to give fate an out, any alternative door to throw open.

Sometimes Charmel thought it was admirable, this unbridled optimism, and it had worked for Thea so far.

But sometimes Charmel worried when she watched her daughter come through the front door after school, after practice—her sweatshirt tied around her hips, her hair curling around her face, so tall and strong, so smart—so sheltered. And who'd done that? Who'd built the soft walls? Worcester Prep, sports camps every summer, the clothes, the movies and dinners, the car when she'd turned sixteen. She and Ron thought they were giving Thea all the things neither of them had had, but standing there in the hospital corridor, Charmel felt fear, fear and remorse. Maybe they'd given her too much, or the wrong things? Thea hadn't seen yet what the world could be. And Thea was making decisions based on her experience, which was nothing.

Oh, once someone screamed "nigger" at her on a street in Baltimore. Once she hadn't gotten a part in the school play because "she didn't fit the stage picture." But now, she was growing into a woman, a Black woman, and Charmel worried that Thea believed life would always be easy. She wished her own mother could have lived just another year to help her talk to Thea. Not that Thea would listen. Charmel thought about how she, at Thea's age, had dismissed her mother, rolling her eyes when she said that the world was a hard place, that struggle was inevitable and necessary.

Thea had some vague idea of medical school, becoming a physical therapist or going into sports medicine. Her grades were solid enough, but Thea had never worked hard to get them. Charmel pointed out to Thea that she'd always hated classes with labs, and her anatomy class had been her least favorite.

"You realize," Charmel told her, "that medical school means years and years of labs, science, anatomy?"

Thea shrugged and pulled a gallon of milk out of the refrigerator. She had just come home from practice, and Charmel handed her that day's raft of college brochures. Glossy covers of happy twenty-somethings tossing footballs, walking autumn campuses under red and yellow trees. The students, too, multi-colored as the leaves, one black, one yellow, one brown, one white.

"If worse came to worse," Thea said, "I could do what you do."

Charmel had been standing at the sink cutting a tomato. She wheeled around to look at her daughter who sat at the island in the kitchen, drinking milk and pecking at her phone, looking bored. "If worse comes to worst, you'll be a judge?" Charmel stopped the bitter laugh that rose up. "That's your plan? That's the way you think the world works?"

"Yeah, if I don't get into Stanford Medical, I'll just go to law school or something. I'll figure it out."

But that's what Ron said, too, "Don't worry. She'll figure it out."

Ron was the most easy-going lawyer she'd ever met. Even when he dealt with high-pressure, high-dollar financial cases, stress never seemed to touched him. He'd tease her that she was a "fretter," and a "super-planner" or a "belt-suspenders-safety pin" person. Had Thea just inherited her father's "it will all work out" approach to the world? It had worked for Ron too, hadn't it? And worked for Thea right up until this injury.

Across the hall, the hospital elevator dinged, and the door slid open. Charmel began her loop again. She looked down at her feet in her brown sandals as they moved over the beige tile floor, looked at the blue toenail polish and thought her mother would have hated it. In some ways, her mother had always remained "a good Black girl from Mississippi," just the way she described herself in her speeches. In most ways, she had not.

Her mother was a force. Charmel and Ron named Thea after her, Dorthea, though her mother went by Dotty. Her mother—a brilliant speaker, strategist, legislator—was one of the first Black women lawyers to come out of Mississippi. And for the rest of her life, her mother categorically refused to ever go back to the state, hated even to fly over it. When Charmel and Ron moved to Delaware, to Wilmington, her mother warned her, "You're getting awful close to that line." Charmel had heard about "that line" all her life—the Mason-Dixon. When they bought the summer house in Rehoboth Beach, her mother said, "All of Southern Delaware was occupied by the Union Army during the Civil War or it would have seceded. Do you know that?"

"I know, Mother," Charmel said, and stopped herself from saying, "I went to law school, too."

When they'd made the decision to live in Southern Delaware full-time, her mother said nothing.

Her mother lived in New York, on the upper East Side, or she had, until she died almost a month ago, February. She died the same week that Thea blew out her ACL, just the day after she got the scholarship to Stanford. Charmel thought it was grief—the grief of her grandmother's death, the grief that Thea had lost the chance to tell her grandmother about the scholarship—that grief had somehow settled in her daughter's knee, though Charmel hadn't said this to anyone because she knew it was crazy. Now she kept imagining a scalpel cutting across Thea's leg, slicing open the smooth brown skin, revealing the lines of the muscle, the white bands of tendon; she imagined this even though the doctor had explained that arthroscopic surgery meant tiny incisions, tiny cameras.

The surgeon had made it all sound benign. "I've done hundreds of them," she said, and then to Thea, "You'll be out in about an hour. You'll go home that day. You'll ice it and rest it and rehab it, and you should be good as new."

That was all Thea heard. She didn't listen at all when Charmel asked, "What are the risks?"

The surgeon pushed one lock of gray-blonde hair behind her ear and sat back in her chair. She ran them all down for Charmel: infection, permanent stiffness, nerve and muscle damage. "We might get in there and find something we didn't expect, but I don't think so. I think this is going to be pretty routine."

*Routine.* She thought of her neighbor, Christine, whose husband, a professor, had died only a week ago. He'd been fine, been out planting beach grass with his class. Was anything routine? As a judge, Charmel had learned to remind herself that a day in court was routine for her, but not for the people who appeared before her. Sometimes they were surprised she was a woman. Maybe they were surprised that she was Black, too. Mostly, they swallowed their surprise, but they didn't swallow their stories; they brought their stories and lay them out before her, tucking the corners, smoothing the wrinkles. "You see, Judge . . ." they'd begin, and then . . . the father in jail or the mother gone before the baby grew, the accidents, addictions, the sicknesses, the untimely deaths, the terrible turns of fate. Maybe all stories were just the way to make sense of the suffering, like her mother's story, "I was a good Black girl from Mississippi."

Charmel had wanted to do that, too, to make the doctor understand—to explain the whole story. "You see, doctor, it's routine for you, but there's a scholarship, and a grandmother, there's unspoiled optimism, and maybe a too-spoiled child, and I'm at sea. And this thing, it might feel routine for you, but it feels like a turning point to me."

## II.

Charmel checked the time—a half hour. Thea had been in there a half hour. She walked back to the waiting room and looked at the big electronic board above the desk. Nothing had changed.

In the corridor, Charmel paced back and forth in front of a line of photographs and text—the history of the hospital from 1916 to the present. For the first few passes, she registered only the outlines, the subjects, but then something made her slow down and look, and actually read. Nurses standing side-by-side in their formal starched caps on a winter day in 1945. 1964 had teenage girls in candy-striped uniforms arranged in front of the Information Desk wearing cat's-eye glasses and sprayed-up hair-dos. She walked to the next picture and her breath caught. Ground breaking on the new wing in 1973. Cranes in the background, the sky overhead promising a storm. But her eyes couldn't slide from the workman in the foreground.

The man looked so much like her Uncle Melvin. He wore an orange hard hat and denim shirt, and he looked up at something out of the frame. He had the same jawline, the same wide stance and broad shoulders, and something about the expression, the lifting of his gaze. She had the thought that she would call her mother and ask if he'd ever been . . . Then she remembered that she couldn't. She lifted her hand to the glass, touched his shoulder. It seemed like a good omen. "Help Thea," she whispered, and saw again Thea's face as the anesthetic took hold.

Her mother named Charmel for her uncles, Charles and Melvin. They'd been Freedom Riders in Mississippi in their late teens. Dotty, born much later, stayed at home with Charmel's grandmother and worried along with her about what would happen to the boys. Dotty and her mother heard the stories from friends, from the radio: the Freedom Riders were being beaten, burned, jailed. Growing up, Dotty's mother pulled her off the sidewalk to let white people pass, told her not to make eye contact or talk back. They'd go to the bathroom before they left the house because the bathrooms for Blacks were dirty and scarce. But Dotty accepted all of this just as her mother had and her grandmother before that. Or that's what she used to say in her motivational speeches, telling the story of her life. "I was a good Black girl from Mississippi, and I accepted these indignities as the lot of Black folks, an accident of birth."

As Dotty told the story, it wasn't her brothers but her own mother who'd changed her mind, changed her life, without meaning to do it. Dotty had come home from school one winter afternoon and the neighbors told her to run, run to the hospital. "They came and took your mama. She's sick!"

Dotty had run all the way, her braids beating against her shoulders, her mouth dry, the brown grass crisp under her feet. No one in her family had ever been to the hospital. Her mother took care of sickness at home with herbs and food and rest.

When she got to the waiting room, Dotty found her mother and the woman who lived next door sitting alone in the section marked "Negroes." Her mother vomited blood into a wash pan in front of her.

Dotty ran to the lady at the desk and said, "My mother is sick. She needs help right away."

"Sit," she said. "When everyone else is taken care of, we'll look at your mother."

Dotty understood what she meant when the woman said "everyone else." She walked back to sit beside her mother and the neighbor, stared down into the washbasin full of blood and up into her mother's tired face. They waited for two more hours before the nurse came out and looked around the empty room, then made her mother stand and walk back behind a door where Dotty couldn't follow.

Three more hours went by, and Dotty and the neighbor sat still in the Negro section with an empty chair and a full washbasin between them. Night had fallen and the neighbor asked Dotty if she was hungry, if she wanted her to go back and get them some supper, but Dotty could only shake her head.

Then time came off the rails. That's what Dotty used to say. When she gave the speech, she would say, "It was 1961 in Mississippi. That was all I knew. And somewhere in the middle of the night the doctor came out and told us that she was gone and we should leave. But when I stood to go and watched his turned back walking toward that door, I screamed like I have never screamed before or since. I screamed, 'You killed her! You killed my mother!' And he did, they did. The woman at the desk, the nurse, the hospital did. Mississippi did. The whole country. All of it. Everyone did. And I meant to stop it."

CHARMEL LOOKED AT THE picture of her uncle, or the man who looked so much like him. She thought of the date—1973. Her mother would already have been working her way through college a piece at a time, setting her sights on getting into law school and out of the south, already on the road that she'd follow until the day she died a month ago, the road to try to right that great wrong.

The man in the picture had her uncle's profile, his jaw, the same slope in his shoulders, but the orange hard hat shadowed his face. It could have been him, she thought. How could she not know this? Her mother would have clucked at her in disbelief. He'd died in the ICU at Crozer-Chester Medical Center, just two hours away from where she stood. Two hours. Maybe he'd been looking for work. Maybe just before he died, he'd come the two hours south to find it before he'd finally succumbed—though Charmel understood this only much later—to a life of pills, cigarettes, whiskey, a life of quiet despair, missed chances, of plans derailed.

MELVIN WAS THE ONE Charmel liked best of her two namesake uncles. Melvin asked her questions like "If you could only eat one flavor of ice cream for the rest of your life, what would it be?" or "Would you rather be able to fly in the sky or to swim without breathing?" Melvin lived with them sometimes for a month or two, or even longer, when he was out of work and out of luck, sleeping on their couch. She loved when Melvin came. Before her mother got home every night, he'd cook them dinner, singing Motown as he chopped and simmered. He'd give Charmel jobs. He called them "her marching orders" and they filled the place with the smell of collards and bacon or beef stew. Melvin laughed with her, conspiratorially, gently. She would tell him how she really felt about her teachers or her chores, and he listened without agenda or demand. When Dotty came through the door, she too seemed lighter, lifted up on the laughter and the smell of the food.

But, most importantly to Charmel, Melvin was the only living soul who ever spoke honestly and spontaneously about Charmel's father. Dotty had three answers for Charmel's questions about her ex-husband and their brief marriage: "He's gone and he's not coming back," "He loved you," "He would have stayed if he could." Her father never made it into her mother's speeches, into her mother's history. Charmel remembered sitting on the floors of libraries and churches with her coloring book and crayons and listening to her mother's talks. Her mother never said her father's name. When Melvin mentioned Barry, Dotty's face slammed shut like a metal lid, and Melvin would catch Charmel's eye with sympathy and change the subject.

WHEN SHE FIRST LEARNED about genetics in high school, Charmel sat up on the edge of the sink and studied her face in the bathroom mirror. She wondered what parts of it were like her father's. She'd never seen a picture of him, but everyone said her eyes were Dotty's, but she was lighter skinned, and her mouth was different, fuller.

She'd tried to ask her mother then, set it up by talking about the science class, said, "What traits do you think I got from . . . you know, him . . . from Barry?"

It was a Friday night and Dotty, just home from work, still in her heels and suit, stood sorting laundry in the bedroom. Melvin had just left the night before, and the rooms felt too quiet.

Charmel asked the question and watched her mother's face cloud as her hands slowed and then stopped, holding a towel out at arm's length like a shield and then dropping it. Her mother got very still and then said in a voice so quiet that Charmel had to almost stop her own breathing to hear it, "You've got his mouth and his strong legs and his laugh. The way you hold your head to the side when you're thinking hard about something, and the way you curl your hands in your lap when you're sad or tired, that's him. But mostly you look like me, or really like your uncles, especially like Melvin."

Charmel didn't recognize the look on her mother's face as she bent down, gathered the laundry, left the room.

TWO NURSES WHEELING an empty bed came by, and Charmel nodded at them without seeing them. Charmel pictured again her mother's face as she walked out of that long-ago bedroom. What was it? Regret? Yes, and anger, but something else. She wanted to ask her mother to tell her the whole story.

Charmel tried to recreate her mother's voice, to remember its exact Southern sweetness and cadence. But the voice was like smoke, disappearing, as her thought moved through it. This was what she grieved, not just the wholesale loss, but the small losses that went with it. She would never hear that voice again. She would never again see her mother toe her shoe off after a long day, or smell her mother's particular smell, a mix of lemon soap and rose-scented face cream, sweet and citrus with something metallic, a brassy edge that was her own beneath it.

Charmel paced past the hospital timeline again and stopped. She wished her mother could see the picture of Melvin, as Charmel now thought of it. Charmel wanted to ask her mother all the questions she hadn't thought to ask when her mother was alive. Had she ever spoken to Barry again? Why had he left? Did her mother ever think about who she might have been had her own mother lived? Charmel did. She wondered how her mother had turned the tragedy into gift.

But was it a gift? Was it true that the moment in the Mississippi hospital had changed her mother's life, or was that an easier story than the realer one? Maybe it wasn't the one tellable tragedy but a lifetime of small indignities—stepping off the sidewalk, holding her eyes down. What was the cost of that?

Charmel had been lucky. Her mother had made sure that Charmel lived in the North, a place that was somewhat better and somewhat fairer. Somewhat. Her mother and uncles had fought for a better world for her, had tried to bring about change. She thought of Thea drifting in her induced sleep. Had Charmel fought hard enough for her?

## III.

An announcement came over the hospital PA system that stuffed animals were twenty-five percent off in the gift shop. Charmel remembered the huge pink bear Ron had bought Thea when she was born. Three feet tall. A monstrosity, Charmel had called it then, and Ron, leaning against the door jamb of the hospital room with the bear in one arm and his eyes fixed on the bassinette at the bottom of the bed, beamed and laughed.

"Where in the hell are we going to put that thing?"

"Right above her crib," Ron said, still laughing, "Or in the rocker and you can lean back on it when you get up in the night to nurse her. It's really soft!"

"Like hell," she said. "Like hell I can!" And though his smile and joy were always contagious, Charmel felt again the edge of panic she had felt then, the sense that the world was changing, slipping out of her control. How would they fit that bear in their tiny apartment already crowded with the stroller and the highchair and everything else? How would this baby fit into their crowded lives? Into her life? What would being a mother mean for everything else she wanted to do? Everything hurt below her waist, and she'd looked up at Ron laughing in the doorway and wanted to scream.

Ron and Charmel had been dating for almost a month when Ron asked, "When do I get to meet the family?" They were sitting in their favorite diner across from the CUNY campus. He caught one of her knees between both of his under the table and squeezed.

"There isn't much family to meet," Charmel said. "It's really just me and my mother, and she's on a kind of speaking tour now, so we'll have to wait until she's back."

"A speaking tour?" Ron raised his eyebrows and lowered the menu.

"She's a lawyer and . . . active in civil rights stuff. She sat for a while on the New York State senate and now she's—"

Ron finished the sentence: "She's Dorothea Greene. Jesus. Your mom is Dorothea Greene, isn't she?" Before Charmel could answer Ron grabbed both her hands, and went on in a rush, "I've seen her speak twice! My God. Your mom is . . . She's a badass, brilliant, she's—"

"She's been speaking a lot lately because, believe me, being a civil rights lawyer doesn't make anyone rich, and—"

"She's Dorothea Greene!"

" —she still has debt from my college tuition, and she's helping me pay for law school, so . . ."

"I saw her speak the first time at the Harry Belafonte Library in Harlem. 'Geography of Discrimination: The History of Black Housing Rights in New York.' Then she came to speak at CUNY last year and I made all my friends go. I said, 'You've got to see this woman!' They were blown away, too. She talked about her life that time."

"'I was a good Black girl from Mississippi,'" Charmel intoned in her mother's Southern accent.

Ron laughed. "Yes!" he said. "Jesus, yes!"

Charmel imagined the meeting, how charmed her mother would be by Ron, not just that he knew her and her work, but by his easy manner and his smile, his quick laugh and quick wit. She pictured a dinner table with the two of them talking nonstop while Charmel faded a little as she still did around her mother in public, becoming "the little girl sitting in the back," the serious, quiet daughter of the firebrand activist.

"A badass." Ron had called Charmel many things, often "beautiful," sometimes "sweet" and "sweetness," but never anything like that, never anything that implied so much spirit and power. Her hands felt suddenly cold, and she wrapped them around the coffee mug wishing it were warmer, wishing she were someone she was not, someone more like her mother.

"She's going to love you," Charmel said with something like resignation, but Ron didn't notice.

"Of course she'll love me!" he boomed. "I'll make damn certain of it!"

CHARMEL WAS GETTING OFF the elevator across from the gift shop when Ron called. He'd had a deposition in Wilmington that morning, and another meeting in the afternoon. He'd said he'd move things around and make it work, but they'd all three agreed he didn't need to come to the hospital, and Charmel herself had been the one to argue that there was no need to have both parents sit in a waiting room. But when the phone rang, Charmel found herself perversely annoyed that he wasn't there.

"She's still in surgery," Charmel said, picking up the call. She heard him take a breath, but he said nothing. "Are you there?" she asked, her voice edged.

"I'm here. I'm here. I figured she would be, but I wanted to check on you. Are you doing okay, baby?" Ron's tone was gentle, and Charmel instantly felt appeased, a little guilty.

"I'm on my way into the gift shop to buy her a pink bear," Charmel said, smiling into the phone.

Ron burst out laughing. "Aw, but I bet they don't have a BIG one. You make sure to get a bear roughly the size of two full grown men, now!"

They laughed together, and Charmel felt the dark worry she'd been carrying lighten a little. She passed the coffee stand in the hallway, and as the good, rich smell hit her, she promised herself a cup on the way back.

"Now I wish you were here," she said, as he said, "I should have come with you."

They laughed again. "No," Charmel said, "it's fine. I just . . . you know how I am. I get to thinking, and then my head goes everywhere. I'm thinking about my mom and my Uncle Melvin. I'm thinking about Thea's whole future. I'm making myself crazy."

"I'll bring home take-out," Ron said. "Thai or something. And Thea will be awake, and the worst will be over."

This was one of the things she loved most about Ron. He believed you could fix problems with Thai food and pink bears, believed that simple things held real comfort. Maybe it was because he'd grown up without lots of material things, or maybe it was just his inborn joy, but sometimes Charmel wished that she could get this quality through some kind of marital transfusion, through osmosis.

"I have to go back," he said. "Will you be okay?"

Charmel pushed open the glass door of the gift shop. "Fine," she said. "I'll call when Thea gets out."

Charmel wondered what mixture created the distinctive smell of hospital gift shops—sweet and vaguely chemical— like roses made with airplane glue. She'd found a small pink stuffed bear that she imagined sold mostly to people wanting gifts for newborn girls. She looked at the bear's sewn mouth and plastic eyes and thought maybe the stuffed bear was a mistake.

Charmel tucked it beneath her arm and looked around for something appropriate for a seventeen-year-old, something graceful and lively, like Thea. Something that bespoke a girl nearly woman, one who might, the very next year decide not to live at home again. A girl who might miss her or not miss her at all, whose future was so totally unknown, so uncertain, but also full of possibility.

The flower arrangements were all stodgy round things, and the books were trash, the rack of scarves and gloves weird and sad. Nothing was right. She finally scooped up candy bars and two little yellow boxes of Whitman's Samplers and put it all on the counter.

The woman behind the counter gathered in the candy and the pink bear, and asked, "Baby girl with a sweet tooth?"

The woman wore a pink volunteer smock, and her eyeglasses swung on a sparkling chain across her chest. She was about the same age her mother would have been, and Charmel wondered if the woman had children and grandchildren, wondered what her life was like. Charmel imagined the woman living alone—saw a dated dark kitchen, an electric tea kettle—her husband passed maybe, her kids grown and gone, living in California. California. She wondered if Thea would still be able to go to Stanford after the surgery.

Charmel looked in the woman's eyes, and then down again, extracting the wallet from her purse. She said, "My baby girl is seventeen. Seventeen! She's having surgery right now. I'm sort of a mess." Even as she said it she thought, *Why the hell are you telling a stranger this?*

"Of course, you are, dear!" the woman said, settling her glasses on the end of her nose and looking at the register. "That's the way all mothers are, just can't help it. We don't want our kids to have any pain. We'd take it all away if we could."

Charmel nodded, but inside she said to the woman, That's just it! I'm wishing her pain. But I'm wishing her the right kind of pain in the right amount. And I'm afraid. I'm afraid because I don't know how much or what kind of pain that is. Her mother's face in the coffin rose in Charmel's mind —cold and arranged, looking nothing like her mother. The smile lines around her eyes smoothed, that H between her brows that was always there when she thought hard, erased. Who was her mother without the hurt she had suffered?

As the woman gave her back the card, she patted Charmel's hand. Charmel looked down at their fingers—old and young, black and white. She noted the large, arthritic knuckles, wondered if the woman's hands ached at night the way her mother's used to. She hoped not. Was it ever okay to wish anyone pain? Or to wish it away?

IV.

**B**ack upstairs, the sign over the desk still said Thea was "In Surgery." Charmel perched on the edge of the orange bucket chair. She sipped the coffee, but it was thin and bitter, nothing like the rich promise of its aroma in the hallway. An orderly emerged from the double doors behind the desk pushing a man in a wheelchair. As they crossed the waiting room, the man groaned loudly in pain and called out. Everyone in the waiting room looked up, stricken, and then looked down again immediately, back to their phones or books. Charmel thought of the way pain connected and isolated. She thought of her friend who finally called her weeks after Dotty's death and said, "I'm embarrassed. I don't know what to say."

Her mother had the heart attack at ten on a Monday morning. The bailiff had put a hand on Charmel's arm before she could call the next case, had whispered in her ear, and though Charmel couldn't remember what she said, she could still feel the woman's breath and hear the sibilance of that sound. A gray day in February, driving North, she couldn't stand either music or silence. She needed human voices, but she didn't want to think about what they were saying. She remembered being seven or eight years old and lying in bed while her mother and Melvin talked in the tiny kitchen of their first apartment. Melvin would lean against the counter, drying, while her mother washed the dishes. The sounds of the glasses and silverware, their words and laughter would float down the hallway and make Charmel feel safe. Crossing into Kent County, Charmel found National Public Radio and turned it down to the point where she could just barely hear it, the reasonable voices soothing, the words lost.

It had snowed the week before, but the white blanket had disappeared, and just the last frozen patches, grey and black with road dirt, melted into the curbs and ditches. Charmel repeated to herself, "No one dies of a heart attack these days" like a mantra.

Later she'd find out that her mother had collapsed as soon as she'd stepped behind the podium at the American Association of University Women meeting. She'd grabbed the microphone in front of her as if to adjust it and then slid down quietly to the ground. She was gone, the EMT said, before they ever got her to the hospital. "A massive heart attack." The man looked at her kindly. "I think she went real quick. I don't think she suffered at all."

CHARMEL FELT A WAVE OF exhaustion wash over her. She hadn't slept well the night before. Around 2:30, she woke up and listened to the rain whispering over the roof and the leaves. Ron snored softly beside her. She heard the cat jump from Thea's bed to the floor and imagined that Thea must have rolled over in her sleep. She thought of Thea's knee, of the surgery.

She thought, *My mother is gone,* because the two thoughts always came together, the two griefs intertwined. The dark weighed on her chest, made it hard to breathe. She rolled toward the window and watched the rain making silver slash marks that Christine and Doug's porch light illuminated. It looked to Charmel like an alphabet that she couldn't read, a message from a world somewhere beyond her.

She imagined her mother's street in New York, the condo buildings lining the East River. Her mother's condo—three stories up, facing the river—had marble floors in the entry way and a fireplace, a nicer place than they'd ever lived in together.

She walked through the empty rooms in her mind. They'd started to clean it all out, to label the furniture, to talk about what to do with the clothes and books. Next month, they'd sell the condo, sell whatever of her mother's they couldn't give away. What would her mother have wanted her to keep, to give to Thea? There was a letter with the will. Dotty wanted Charmel to have the plain gold wedding ring that Barry had slid on her hand at the wedding. Charmel started to slip it on her own finger and then felt strange about that trespass and slipped it back into its box.

Thea was to get a silver spoon that had somehow come down from Charmel's grandmother that was stowed in the same drawer. Charmel opened the disintegrating box and pulled the spoon from the yellowing cotton. Where had her grandmother ever gotten such a thing? As poor as they were, where could she have bought or been given something so relatively valuable? She resettled the spoon and realized that the story, too, was gone.

SITTING IN THE WAITING ROOM, Charmel kept twisting the pieces of her life, holding them up in the light and watching them fall into new patterns as though the past were a kaleidoscope. Then she felt the pieces settle in a pattern she'd never seen before. Her mother's face came into focus through a new lens, and she heard the story her mother told as if she were in the back of one of those long-ago rooms, but grown now, a mother herself.

And she understood. Her mother had never been able to overcome that moment in the Mississippi emergency room though she'd worked to do it her whole life. She'd fought and organized and legislated and spoke. She'd tried to fix the laws, the historical record, the minds of thousands of people. She'd tried to fix the world. But had never been able to fix the thing that her own mother's death had first broken: her own fear, her loneliness, her anger, her pain.

Charmel swallowed hard. She felt a wave of sympathy and sorrow wash over her as she saw her mother now, not as her "badass" mother, but as a woman whose life had been painful and complex.

She wanted to talk to her mother more than she'd ever wanted anything in her life. She wanted to sit with Melvin on the fire escape and look into his face. She wanted to sit at the kitchen table with Ron and understand everything that he meant to her. The enormity of her own life and of all the lives that touched hers, the longing to go back into the past and understand, pulled her under like a wave. Then she thought about Thea, the future, dragging the past forward.

The air thinned to nothing; she felt faint.

Charmel took a breath, another. She looked around the waiting room. You're here, she told herself. She took another sip of the cold, terrible coffee. She looked around. A woman knitting. A man with two teenaged boys, the boys' long legs sprawling across the uncomfortable chairs, their eyes glued to their phones. She imagined telling Ron about the room, the chairs, the people; imagined him asking her, "What did you do while you waited?"

But how could she explain? And what would she tell him when he asked, "What did you do in the hour while you waited?"

Paced.

Saw a picture of someone who may or may not have been my uncle.

Bought useless gifts and bad coffee.

Realized that all stories get lost and changed.

Worried the future.

Grieved the past.

Found my mother too late.

The woman at the information desk came over and touched her shoulder. Charmel started, blinked back the tears, looked up at her "Your daughter's out of surgery," the woman said. "She's in the recovery room. Do you want to go back?"

# EXPLAIN

I'm never like this. Anyone here will tell you I'm the nicest person and great with the patients, especially the tough ones. It's my superpower. The worse the patient, the better I am at getting around their defenses. And I'll tell you a secret, most of the time it's not that hard. They're people. They want something and they're scared. All you do is figure out what those two things are: the scared-of thing and the want thing.

But today went bad, really it started bad and just got worse. That's not an excuse. I admit it. I lost it. I told the guy who wanted to go to John's Hopkins that he should go to hell. I pitched that woman's purse against the wall and called her a "goddamn junkie," and I said things I shouldn't have, even to Sue, the attending, who didn't deserve it.

It's probably going to end in some kind of formal reprimand, isn't it? It's going to end up in my file, and it'll maybe cost me my job and there's nothing I can do. Because that's the deal, right? If you're an ER nurse, you're never supposed to lose your cool. Not when they bring in a three-year-old girl whose mother left her in a closed car in ninety-five degrees for "just a half hour." Not when your sixth-grade teacher codes on the stretcher in front of you.

And when the three-year-old girl, who's as blonde as my daughter, ends up with brain damage which you knew she would because it was way more than a half hour, and when you talk to Mr. Sterne, your sixth grade teacher's wife and tell her what a wonderful teacher he was and how he changed your life, no one puts a sheet in your file that says that you held that lying mother while she cried, even though you wanted to shake her, or that you lied yourself to help Mr. Sterne's wife feel a little better, because, to be honest, he was just a so-so teacher who probably didn't like his job or the kids much.

And that's the thing—I love my job. Most days I look forward to coming in, even the weekends. Even in the summer when we have three times the patient load and we're always short staffed. This weekend just got off on the wrong foot. Bad, like I said.

My daughter, Emma, she's five. Because I'm working over July 4th, she's staying with her dad. His name's Travis, Travis Waller. Maybe you've seen the white trucks around with the cartoon cockroach all legs up on the side and Waller Exterminators in red. "If bugs make you holler, just call Waller." Exactly. That's him.

We split a year ago, and I'm not so comfortable yet with all of this, the fact that she'll be doing the sparklers and fireworks with him, and I won't see any of it, won't be part of her memory. Not that any of that is Travis's fault. Don't misunderstand. He's a good man. Strong. Quiet. A good dad, too. The split was my fault.

I expect you've heard about it because, well, you know how this place is. You could call it General Hospital instead of Beebe for all the rumors, more of a soap than anything on TV. But I want you to know that the doctor, I won't say his name, but you probably know it, he told me he was separating from his wife, which it turned out he wasn't, and told me he was interested in something long term which I believed. Idiot. Of course, I was married, so . . . But then, he was a doctor, and you know how that can be, having the patients in common, having a shorthand with each other. He had this dream of taking me to Europe, to Italy. We dreamt a lot of dreams. You know the way it happens. You're with someone every day and you count on them, and they count on you. The next thing you know, you start really talking to that person, and they listen and . . . Anyway, I was a fool.

But Travis, my husband—ex—he comes over to get Emma and she's all dressed in her shorts and white sandals; she's got her little pink suitcase and she's excited because Travis told her all the fun things they'll do and about the fireworks, and I can't help but feel this just pulling at me. So, I walk them out to the car and I'm doing okay, I'm not crying, just telling her I love her and I'll see her on Tuesday. Travis buckles her into the car seat and I kiss her and then, as we walk around the back of the car, Travis touches my arm and says "Tina" and looks at me and says he needs to tell me something.

He's been seeing someone for a while, and he thinks that it's time she meets Emma because he's feeling pretty serious. Megan. That's her name. I picture her with light green eyes and freckles across her nose because I knew a girl named Megan in high school who looked like that. He's still holding my arm and I look down at his hand, at his square fingernails all clipped and neat. He says he's going to introduce this Megan as a friend, but he wanted me to know just in case and because he didn't want me to find out from Emma, he didn't think that would be fair.

Fair.

Can you imagine? After what I'd done. He's a good man, you see? He's just good, and I wish I could do more than admire that, because he's a good dad, too, and I wish . . . I always wish . . . but there it is.

I don't say anything. I just shake my head and the tears are coming now because I can't hold them back and I grab the hand on my arm and hold it tight and choke out something about wanting his happiness and then I let him go and I walk inside and I wave with my back turned because I don't want them, either of them, to see me crying. When I come in, I stand at the counter and I can't see because I'm crying so hard, and Snowy, that's the cat, she jumps up and spills my coffee all down my favorite scrubs.

So it started there and, though you think you'd have nowhere to go but up, it just kept going down and down.

When the shift started, everything was a wreck. The monitor wires were all braided into the blood pressure tubing and the supply carts were low. I know. It happens. People get busy, but today it felt like one impossible mess after another, like the whole world was a mess and nothing would ever be fixed or happy or whole again.

Then, the entire time I'm unbraiding the wires and stocking the carts, some part of my brain is chewing away at this woman, this Megan, and what she looks like and what she does for a living and how skinny she is and pretty and young. I don't know any of this, of course. But I imagine her holding Emma's hand and the three of them looking up at the fireworks from a picnic blanket and I can't stop.

Usually, I can stop. That's one of the things I love about being in the ER. The shift starts and everything else gets put on hold, you don't think about anything else except the people in front of you and what you have to do that very minute.

But not today. Today I kept getting trapped in my head. First, we had Mrs. Shipley who went up to CCU with another possible heart attack—the fourth time in as many months, God bless her—and I thought about how she never has anyone with her, no husband, no kids, and I wondered if that would be me, you know, a few years down the line. I thought about being alone, if I never find anyone and Emma moves away. I thought about this guy, Brian, who never returned my call even though we'd had such a good night.

Then the professor comes in, the John's Hopkins guy. He plucks my last nerve from the moment I hear his voice. Insisting that this was a "po-dunk little shithole" hospital and that we better airlift him to John's Hopkins. For a sprained wrist and road rash. Really! The wrist wasn't even broken. It wasn't even warm, but he wouldn't let us do an X-ray because only John's Hopkins' doctors can read an X-ray. He's a Marketing Professor at the University and he kept saying he was a doctor, which he is, of course, but not the kind that can fix a wrist, so why keep saying it?

It ought to be illegal to come to the beach on the July 4th weekend and rent a bike when you haven't been on a bike in fifteen years. Right? Why do they have to drive two hundred miles to fall off their bikes here? Fall off your damn bike at home.

But I didn't blow up then, not even close.

I kind of felt sorry for him even, along with all the other feelings. When I walked in the room, he was looking down at the white ice pack cupped in his hands like he was scared. It reminded me of the way Emma had looked at Snowy when she first found him, a white kitten in the drainage ditch behind the house. She brought him to me cupped in her hands and didn't take her eyes off him, like he might disappear if she stopped looking.

Also, I kept comparing the professor's drama to Jeff, our neighbor's son, who died last fall. He was also in a bike accident, also on Route 1. I was in here that day, when he came in, though I didn't know then who he was. He'd been wearing a big black sports watch and I had to take it off and I suddenly thought that when he'd put it on to go out for his ride, he'd never imagined somebody else's hands taking off his watch. Then I noticed that the stopwatch was still running, ticking off the seconds like he was still on the bike, still pedaling toward the bridge with the dunes beside him and the sun on his arms. I hit the button and the time stopped and for a second I couldn't breathe.

Anyway, I was in the middle of dealing with the professor—cleaning the asphalt out of his knees and thinking about Jeff while the professor threatens me with lawyers and talks down the hospital and medicine and the nursing profession—when Sue pokes her head in to tell me that Lilly's back. I don't know if you know the Lilly stories. She comes in about twice a month trying to get us to give her OxyContin. You should see this lady.

When you look from a distance, you'd think she was something—a Coach purse, country club clothes. But when you get close, you can see your mistake. The skin on her face and arms just hangs, her color's wrong. But it's really the eyes that give it away, constricted pupils—she can't keep them still, can't focus, and they're dead when you look at her, flat, like a burnt-out match.

If I'm on, I'm always the one to deal with her because, like I said, I'm great with the difficult patients. I talk to her; she tells me about her family. She says I remind her of her daughter. But here's the scary thing. She—Jesus—she reminds me of my mom. My mom's gone now. She was a drunk, not an addict, but it's the same really. Same promises, same lies and games. Although Lilly's a smart one, cagier than my mom. And today—today she came up with a doozy. She was calling 911 from inside the Emergency Room and telling dispatch she needed to be picked up by ambulance and taken to another hospital. Telling them that the staff at Beebe was abusing her. Perfect, right? Sue and I even laughed a little. "No one wants to be here today!" That's what Sue said.

So, you know, I start out calm. I tell Lilly she's got to give me the phone. I tell her that she has two choices: she calls again and we admit her to the Psych ward or she gives me the phone and we find her a rehab. Now she's been in rehab before, but I'm thinking maybe this time it'll stick. I'm thinking maybe we can find an open bed, even on this short notice because it's a holiday weekend. She's got a death grip on her big white purse, pulling it into lap and she's shaking her head, licking her lips obsessively even though they're already cracked and bleeding.

"Give me the phone, Lilly," I say. I sit down across from her. I cross my legs. I tell her, "I can wait."

She looks at me and her eyes get hard, and she says, "You got no plans this weekend? No where to go?"

"Just working." Even as I say it, I feel it in the pit of my stomach. I see Emma again and her pink suitcase and her meeting Megan and the fireworks bursting over their heads like it's a movie and the little family they're going to make stands there happy and together under the sparkling lights and I'm sick. I'm sick thinking about it.

Lilly's still looking at me and she stops licking her lips and gets still and—just like she can see it go through me, like there's some kind of running ticker across my forehead—she kind of hisses, "You'll never get what you want. I will. If you won't give it to me, I'll get it somewhere else. But you? You'll never get it. Never."

It was like she'd turned on a fire hose inside me and no one was holding it. Like if I didn't move I . . . and I thought of that stopwatch running and of Emma and the fireworks exploding. I stood up and yanked Lilly's purse away from her and fished out the phone, an iPhone, and I slammed it onto the floor then kicked it across the room. I threw the purse against the wall with both hands, and I called her a junkie, a goddamned junkie. All the time I'm doing it, she's looking at me with this little smile, like this was what she wanted, and she looks just like my mother. Just like my mother looked when she was drunk enough to need more booze, but not so drunk that she would pass out. It felt like my dead mother predicting my future, haunting me. *You'll never get what you want.* So, I started to run.

I don't know where the hell I thought I was going, but out, at least, away. I get close to the room where the professor is still lecturing Sue even as she's treating him, even as she's bandaging him up, and Sue's trying to be nice. I hear her say she is a real doctor, with this little laugh, and that he doesn't have any nerve damage. I can't take it. I can't listen to it and I turn and go through the curtain and I yell at him that he can go to John's Hopkins or hell for all anyone cares if he'll just get out of the ER and never come back. Sue starts to say something—and this is the part I really regret—I call her a fucking idiot, a fool to put up with his B. S.

Then I'm going again, running out through the waiting room, where there's a case of pink eye and someone holding a dishtowel on a bloody hand, and I make it out to the parking lot and I run to my car and I stand there with no keys in my hand, just looking in at the steering wheel, at the little pink pony Emma left on the floor behind the seat. Suddenly I don't know what to do. The sun beats down; the heat seeps through the soles of my shoes. I'm breathing hard. I put my hands on the hot roof, and I feel them burning and I want it to burn. I want it to raise blisters.

I think about driving right to Travis's and asking him to reconsider, to try again. I can't do that. I think maybe I'll just go home and crawl in bed and never get out again, but I can't do that either and I have no keys and I can't go back in to get them and then I realize I've started screaming. No words, just one loud sob.

I look up and Sue is coming across the parking lot, her long blonde braid bouncing behind her, and she doesn't look angry; she looks scared and relieved, and she puts her arm around me and brings me in here. To face the music, I guess. To apologize.

Explain? Okay then, to explain.

# BRIAN'S HOUSE

Brian sat on the couch eating a roast beef hoagie, waiting for the Phillies to rally against the Pirates in the eighth. Bowtie curled beside him with one paw on Brian's leg. Every so often Brian pulled a piece of meat out of the sandwich or grabbed a potato chip from the bag and tossed it to the dog who sat up and gobbled it in loud smacks and then returned to his original position, neither begging nor refusing, just looking intently from Brian to the Phillies and back again.

"You're a dignified beast, aren't you?" Brian rubbed the dog behind the ears, and the dog lowered his head. "You're not a whiner, and you root for the Phils." He threw the dog another chip just as César Hernández lobbed one from second base to the plate for an easy third out.

"Bases loaded and the Pirates got nothing to show for it." If Jeff and Sylvie had been there with him, they'd have been on their feet, cheering and high fiving. But Brian just nodded. When the commercial came on, he got up—not to celebrate, just to go to the bathroom.

The dog followed him down the hall and stood beside him, intently watching the stream of piss.

The mirror he'd bought to hang above the sink three years ago when he moved in still rested behind the faucets. He bent to look at the place where he'd nicked his chin shaving, splashed his face with water, then grabbed the hand towel that he'd draped over the doorknob. The dog nudged the door open with his head and looked back for Brian.

"I know," Brian said. "You don't have to give me that look. I should hang the mirror."

Sylvie used to give him a hard time about it. "You don't need an engineering degree, Bri. It's one nail."

Part of it was that he'd never been sure he liked the mirror. Painting the walls was the same. He'd go into the hardware store and grab handfuls of the color strips in the paint aisle, but when he brought them home, he had no idea what might be right, what he might want.

Brian had always imagined when he'd found the right person, they would buy a house together, like his parents had, like Jeff and Sylvie had. He and whoever she was would decide together—mirrors, paint, dishes, curtains. There'd be wedding gifts and trips to Home Depot or whatever.

Jeff was the one who encouraged Brian to buy the house. He'd actually taken Brian out to lunch one afternoon to talk him into it, interrupted their lab work and said, "Come on. I have a pitch I want to make to you."

He had all the reasons ready. Brian had money from an inheritance, and he was making a good salary. The University matched down payments up to $5,000 for employees who bought a home near their campus. It was a tax write-off. Real estate would only get more expensive near the beach, especially with all the new developments going up. It was an investment.

"But what if my future wife hates the house?"

"Then you'll sell it, make a pile of money, and buy a house she loves."

Brian pointed at him with a French fry. "You haven't gone into real estate behind my back, have you?"

Jeff laughed and shook his head. "Jesus, no."

"Sylvie? Has she dropped teaching the first grade for hustling houses at the beach?"

"No! This is totally altruistic. We saw the house when we were driving around, and at first, we thought of it for Regina, but then we thought of you. It just seemed perfect! Close to work and you got that inheritance and now . . ."

"You and Sylvie have been working out how I should responsibly spend it. You and Sylvie have talked it all through, and you're 'fixing me up' with a house? Are you sure she doesn't know some gorgeous single teacher you could fix me up with instead?"

Remembering the conversation, Brian felt his chest constrict. He touched the head of the dog beside him. "You miss him, too. Don't you?"

Brian dreaded watching the dog, had done it only because Sylvie was desperate and looking for reasons to stay home. Some girlfriends had planned a road trip they wanted her to go on, the ferry to New Jersey and then New York, beaches, shows, fun. She said she wasn't ready for fun, but they were pressuring her, albeit nicely, using the phrase "almost a year" over and over.

"Like my suggesting you let go of the clothes," Brian said gently.

Then she blew out a long breath. "And I wasn't ready for that either! You're right. I'm not ready to go anywhere."

"No! That's not what I'm saying at all. This isn't forever. It's one weekend. One." He'd looked out the window in the direction of her house like he could will her to listen to him. "It's a great idea! I'll even watch Bowtie. You need this, Sylv. One weekend. Come on."

She'd dropped the dog off with a long list of instructions and food and toys and phone numbers. When he'd seen her at the door, he'd done a double take. She'd lost weight even since they'd had lunch a month ago.

"Are you eating?" he asked, as he kissed her cheek and grabbed Bo's leash.

"And hello to you, too!" she said. There was a laugh in her voice but not in her eyes. Then he noticed that she had on a blue blouse he'd never seen before, and new jeans.

"You look really nice," he said. "Beautiful. It's just . . . you're thinner than—"

She gave him a look. "Good save."

As she talked him through the lists and instructions, Brian had the thought that she did look beautiful, that she wouldn't be single for long. The thought made him obscurely angry and protective. Whoever the guy was, Brian thought, he would tear him apart if he hurt her.

"Are you listening to me?" she said, mildly amused and exasperated.

"Yes! Don't give him more than one bone chewy in a day or he throws it up."

"Not just the bone chewy! He throws up everything and he throws it up everywhere. I swear, you'll regret bone chewy number two. This is the voice of experience!"

After she'd left, Brian closed the door and looked down at the dog. "Don't even ask for a second bone chewy. Whatever that is. And don't you dare run off or get sick or do anything on my watch you wouldn't do on hers. Do you hear me? I'm not kidding!"

The dog had cocked his head, barked once, and wandered off to the kitchen.

THAT WEEK BRIAN GOT UP early every day to walk the dog before he went to the lab. He left work early to get another walk in before dinner. He'd surprised himself with how much he had come to love their neighborhood rambles. Bo pulled him down streets he'd never thought to wander before, cataloguing smells, barking at squirrels in the branches and rabbits under hedges. Brian liked seeing the sunrise climb behind the trees, the wet grass at dawn, liked the sound of lawn mowers and the kids playing in driveways in the long summer evenings.

For the first time since he'd moved in, he met some of his neighbors. A beautiful East Asian woman with a killer smile and great legs who ran in the mornings and always stopped to pet the dog. The first morning, after they parted ways, he thought he might ask her out, but the next time they saw each other, before he could say anything, she mentioned she lived at the end of the cul-de-sac and was married to the doctor with the ERDOC license plate.

She stuck out her hand and flashed that smile, "Meera Tancredi."

"I met your husband. Mark, right?" Brian said. He noticed that her handshake was real and strong, not the perfunctory thing some women did.

The next morning, Mark and Meera were out in the drive together, both headed to work. He waved as they passed, but they called him over.

"We're having a fight," she laughed.

"A discussion," Mark corrected.

"Okay, we're having a discussion. Do you think it's weird—"

"Stop right there! You're leading the witness! Corn on the cob: around or across."

Brian burst out laughing. "Across. Of course! Who would eat it around? You'd get it all over your face."

Mark fist bumped him, and Meera shook her head.

While the three of them laughed, Bo sniffed around their feet and went from one to the other for pets. The conversation felt so easy that Brian kept coming back to it through the course of the day and smiling.

Before having the dog, Brian's life had revolved around work, the gym, whatever woman he happened to be dating. He walked from his door to his car, his car to his door. Bowtie changed all that. They ambled up and down the sidewalks of the development and each day Brian let it take a little longer.

Sometimes, in the early morning dark, he could smell coffee from somewhere. He noticed which houses had lights on in the upstairs windows. Often another dog barked behind a closed door, and Bowtie barked back. As the sky grayed and streetlights flickered off, Brian would turn back toward home reluctantly. Bo seemed reluctant, too. Brian found, to his surprise, that he loved his neighborhood—the quiet streets, the flowers around the mailboxes, loved noticing out-of-state license plates or a different welcome flag.

Sometimes he would forget that Jeff was gone, and he'd take note of something to tell him, the whippet-thin guy with the Italian racing bike, the Japanese maples surrounding a rock garden. Then the truth of Jeff's death would blow through him.

THE PHILLIES WERE BATTING the top of their line-up. Not that Brian could bring himself to care. When he watched with Jeff and Sylvie, sometimes with Regina, they cared. They were loud enough some nights that his neighbor— the house was semi-detached—would complain about the noise. That seemed like years ago. He thought about calling Regina, checking in. Then he felt awkward about it all. *You fucked that up but good*, he thought. He watched as another runner rounded third.

"They're going to win," Brian said out loud, trying to feel something about that fact. "I can't believe they're going to pull this out." Then, he looked down at the dog, rested his hand between the dog's ears. In three days, Brian would give Bo back. He imagined how it would feel when the dog was gone. Waking up alone, coming home from work and opening the door to the empty house.

"I have to get out of here," he said, and the dog shifted to look him in the eye. "Where will I go?"

Bowtie whined. "You're right," Brian said. "Anywhere that's not here." Any-fucking-where. He threw his eyes around him—the beige furniture, the blank walls—snd he was suddenly furious at Jeff and Sylvie for talking him into buying the place, furious at himself for doing it. The fury felt like carbon steel, dark and metallic. He could almost taste it.

He let it fill him until he cursed loud enough to scare the dog, who jumped down and stood in front of him with his head cocked. Then Brian stood up himself and started to pace. It was almost a relief to feel something so solid, so clear.

He'd always known what the house was. He'd just never let himself see it until that minute. A stage set for a life he didn't have.

*I'll sell the house*, he thought, and then he said, "I'll take a leave of absence from work. I'll go somewhere warm, somewhere far. Tahiti, maybe. I'll live in a shack by a beach."

He could do it. He looked down at Bo who was pacing beside him. "I could, you know. There's nothing holding me. No one who needs me to stay."

He closed his eyes. He felt the house around and above him like a weight. He felt the air heavy in his lungs. He wondered how he'd ever gotten so alone.

# DIVIDE

They'd seen each other last at the July 4th party his parents hosted every year. His father manned the grill, beer in hand, laughing too loudly to his Uncle Ron and the semicircle of men in dad shorts standing away from the smoke. His mother bustled back and forth in the kitchen, talking to his Aunt Charmel and Brian from down the street, lifting pot lids, stirring, giving Julian orders. She shoved a stack of plates in his hands and gestured to the porch.

Julian stood in the door and scanned the crowd, the neighbors and families who came to the party every year for as long as he could remember. There was the usual group of little kids tearing around playing cornhole and tag. The weather was perfect, unusually cool with enough breeze to lift the little flags his mother had planted around the gazebo.

That's where Thea sat, perched on the steps, scrolling through something on her phone and looking bored. She and Julian had seen each other at events like this since they'd been the little kids racing around the yard—her parents' annual Christmas party, Super Bowl Sunday, birthdays. She had on torn jean shorts, a blue tee shirt, and oversized sunglasses.

Julian stared at her a moment, then set places at the picnic table and walked across the lawn. He had intended to sit down beside her, but when she looked up, he couldn't see her eyes behind the sunglasses, and he felt suddenly awkward. They had something like a conversation:

Why do California schools start so late?

"I don't know. Maybe because it's hot?"

How weird it was that they wouldn't be going back to Worcester Prep again. "Definitely."

Julian scrambled through topics they had in common, trying to find something, anything, that might be interesting. Somehow, he froze up and turned into some shy middle school idiot around Thea. She crossed her legs, and he looked at the taut muscle line between her quad and hamstring.

"Nice Vans," he said. And when she laughed, he didn't know if she had caught him leering or if she was mocking his lame attempt at game. "When I used to skateboard, I bought—"

"I got them yesterday." They both stared at her shoes for an awkward moment, then his father called him, and Julian turned on his heel and headed for the grill, cursing under his breath. He and Thea had played together as kids. They'd gone to the same school. He'd even dated Kaitlyn Greer, one of her friends. Why was he such a fucking mess around her?

SHE TEXTED AT 9:00 A.M. his time during the second week they were on campus. You up? A month since the Fourth of July party, they'd both left for college because their teams—Stanford volleyball for her, Dartmouth lacrosse for him—started practices before classes.

He caught his breath and lifted his eyebrows, and then realized she probably sent it accidentally. Hey. Yeah. It's 9 here. He added a smiley and then erased it and then added it again.

She texted, Oops, Forgot with an emoticon shrugging its shoulders.

In high school, they'd communicated only about practical things—rides to school, practice, homework. They'd talked on the phone exactly once, when they were fifteen, and though he remembered it, he was positive she didn't.

Julian wrapped his hand around the Starbucks cup to keep warm. The Starbucks was as quiet as the campus in early August. Dartmouth had sent Julian emails to warn him that it would be hot in New Hampshire, that he'd want to make sure to bring a fan for his room, and to hydrate during practice. But when he got to campus, he realized it was much colder than Delaware, and there was no humidity. At night, it went down to the upper forties. He wore a sweatshirt to bed and woke up freezing.

Julian stared down at the three flashing dots, and when they stopped, he wrote, How's CA? You doin OK? The rhyme made the phrase bounce around his head until it sounded childish. CA/OK. CA/OK. Julian wondered if Thea felt like he had these last two weeks. Like he was trying hard every minute. The practices were ballbusters, and at night, he'd go over in his head all the mistakes he made, all the plays he blew. Off the field, he felt awkward, like he couldn't put two sentences together without feeling self-conscious.

If Thea had ever felt like that, she never showed it. His mother always called her "self-possessed," and it was the perfect word for her. She didn't seem to worry as much as he did about what other people thought. In high school, anyone she was friends with instantly got cooler because she liked them. She hung out with band geeks and emo kids, and anyone she felt like.

Maybe he'd looked the same way from the outside. A jock with the lacrosse team, an emo dude and artist with the newspaper and yearbook staff; his friend, Nimesh, had even called him "an honorary Asian."

"What do you mean 'honorary,' asswipe? I'm Indian! I'm like three-quarters Indian. My grandparents are from Jaipur."

So far, college had felt like that, like he was inside but outside at the same time. After the first week, he wondered why he'd chosen Dartmouth, or why Dartmouth had chosen him. Was it their attempt at diversity? The Indian kid who plays lacrosse? He'd said as much to Nimesh on the phone and Nimesh scoffed, "Right! It had nothing to do with them scouting you at the tournaments or your 4.0 or anything!"

Behind Julian, someone opened the door and let in a blast of cold air, and the barista pointed beyond his head and sang out a name and an order. The people behind the counter seemed to know everyone, everyone but him, of course.

His phone lit up again. Thea.

`I just saw this woman who looks so much like your mom!`

Julian read the sentence twice. What should he say to that? Though he knew Thea was sitting in her dorm room, he imagined her instead sitting at the picnic table on his back porch, looking down at the phone with a bored face, waiting for a reply. He felt like there was a language beneath the language that he'd never learned, that he needed to know immediately. He wrote `wow` and then erased it. *For Christ's sake*, he thought. *She's a friend. Text your friend.*

`Weird. She's def not there. Why are you awake to see mom2?`

This time she texted back right away. `Don't know. I can't seem to get on the Cali clock.`

Julian sat back in the rickety chair and took a last long drink of his coffee. He had to go if he was going to get to practice on time. He couldn't think of anything that didn't sound forced. Finally, he put the phone in his pocket and walked out.

But he thought about the exchange the rest of the day, and the next afternoon, he texted her— `Hope you slept in` and a smiley face. He rolled his eyes at himself as he pressed send, fully expecting that he would hear nothing, or she'd give it a "thumbs up" and the conversation would be over.

Instead, Thea texted back asking him how practices were going. It started a long series of questions over days—about food, sleep, coaches, what they thought they might major in. They wrote paragraphs, something Julian had never done before in his life. They'd text all day, an extended conversation that wove through practices, dinners, team meetings. They talked about everything—the weird way her coach said "lah" instead of "law," his hikes at The Bema and Moose Mountain, the food on campus, missing the ocean. Late at night, reluctantly, Julian would finally text `Going to hit it` and she'd text back `Goodnight`

Sometimes he'd stare at the word and feel sure they were a couple, or they'd be one as soon as they actually saw each other. Sometimes he'd put the phone down beside the bed and decide he had to stop doing this, thinking this, because in a few weeks she would start ghosting him. His friend Danny had been dating a girl in high school, and when they went to college, she just slowly disappeared. She never broke up with him exactly, but she stopped returning his texts and calls. It had seemed to Julian a brutal thing to do to someone.

Not leaving, but not staying either. He realized then that it was what his dad was doing, holding himself just outside of the family—working shift after bullshit shift at the hospital—and when he was home, he was always in the basement talking on the phone to his side thing. Julian shook his father out of his head and scrolled back through Thea's texts until he fell asleep.

Then one night, instead of texting goodnight, Thea called. They'd ended up talking for two hours.

"Why didn't I ever really know you when we lived five minutes from each other?" They were whispering because their roommates were asleep. They were both living with other freshmen on their teams. She said hers was "pretty nice." Julian's was a guy from New Jersey he'd met a couple of times playing on the travel team. Already he could tell they'd never really be friends because the kid loved to party and had put up pictures of himself doing a handstand on a keg with the tap in his mouth.

Julian curled into the side of his bed, the sheets pulled over his head, the phone a blue glow against the cinderblock wall. "We've always known each other," he said, "like since we were in diapers."

"Yeah," she said, "but you know what I mean."

Julian wanted to tell her the truth, that he knew everything he could about her. He wanted to say, "You hate water chestnuts, scratchy tags in sweatshirts, and people who call everyone 'dude.' You love animals, especially elephants and Bengal cats (which your mom won't let you have) and when we were in middle school, you were going to be a vet. Your favorite car is a 1968 Mustang. You used to visit your badass grandmother—that's what your dad called her—in New York for long weekends and you said you went to shows and restaurants and shopping and I pictured it all: you moving under those tall buildings, the doormen, the taxis. At your grandmother's funeral, you looked the saddest I've ever seen you look, and I wanted to say something, anything, to make you understand that I cared, but I couldn't think of anything."

Instead, he said, "Your favorite time of day is 12:34."

"What?" she laughed. "How do you know that?"

"You said it once."

"When?"

"I can't remember," he lied. He could still hear her voice from the front seat, her mom driving them to practice on a Saturday when his mom was at the hospital. He'd been staring at her profile. "Your favorite color is red."

"Yours is blue," she said quietly. "I remember you always wanted the blue properties when we played Monopoly."

Even though he'd known her for so long, had grown up right beside her, it was the things he didn't know that he kept thinking about. Was she a virgin? He thought so, but he couldn't be sure. Senior year, she'd dated one of the guys who worked with Julian on the yearbook and newspaper. They'd broken up in the spring, but he wondered if they still talked. He was an artist who took pictures and drew cartoons, a tall guy with dark, trimmed beard who looked older than seventeen. Julian remembered seeing them together at a dance, seeing this guy lean down and whisper something in Thea's ear that made her laugh. As they were laughing, they'd leaned their foreheads together. Julian had stood transfixed by the intimacy of the moment.

ONE NIGHT IN EARLY SEPTEMBER, while she was walking back from her late-night Biology lab, ten at night her time, Thea started talking about how privileged they both were, about growing up around their parents, their parents' friends, doctors and lawyers, professionals. "My sociology professor, she assumes—because I'm black and here on an athletic scholarship—my parents are poor. When she talks about privilege in class, she always looks at me meaningfully, and I get so pissed. Bitch, my mother's a judge! You don't know shit about me."

"Yeah, my mother's a doctor and my father's an asshole," Julian said, and almost immediately regretted it. He laughed weakly. He was sitting on the steps of the dorm, the cold of the concrete seeping through his jeans. "I mean, that's harsh, but . . ."

"You don't have to take it back," Thea said. She was quiet a long moment and he heard her footsteps on the sidewalk across the continent. "Why do you think that? What did he do?" she said.

"Oh, it's just that lately, you know—" Then he stopped. Wisps of cloud cut the half-moon; a breeze rose in the pine trees. "Look. Fuck it. Here it is. He cheated on my mom. They don't think I know, but I knew before she did. I heard him on the phone in the basement, that stupid voice he used.

When my mom found out, she walked around for weeks looking like the world was over. She lost like twenty pounds."

He heard Thea's footsteps stop. "My God," she said, "I remember when your mom . . . I can't even believe it. Uncle Mark? That's insane."

Uncle Mark. He heard their whole history. "I shouldn't have said anything. Please don't tell your—"

"No!" she said. "I won't. I promise."

The arm holding the phone to his ear felt heavy. Julian wished she were sitting beside him, looking at the same sky. He could imagine her expression, the way her mouth disappeared into a thin line when anything hurt or upset her. "You don't need to know all this."

"I'm glad you told me."

"My parents would die if they knew I knew. They'd fucking shame-spiral if they knew I told you."

"So when did all this happen?"

"I found out right before prom, and then I guess my mom found out a couple weeks later. They tried all summer to act normal, but . . . ." Julian heard a shout come from somewhere to the left, and then the music turned up loud.

"You must have been glad to leave for school."

"Sort of." He flashed to the day his parents had moved him into his dorm room. His father lifting the crate of lacrosse stuff from the back of the car, saying "You are going to have the time of your life." His father's face had filled with a sad-ness Julian hadn't seen before. Would his father miss him? Julian had wondered what their life would be like without him in the house. He'd wondered if his dad even loved his mom anymore, if his dad loved the woman he talked to in the basement. He wondered, too, if he loved his dad. What that even meant.

Thea pulled in a deep breath. "I'm blown away," she said. "He's always seemed so devoted to your mom, so kind. He took good care of me when I hurt my knee, and when my grandmother died, he stopped to check on us a lot."

"Yeah," he said, "that's the thing. He's always been, you know, *the man*. He helps everyone. Everyone thinks he's the shit. And I don't even know when it started, but he's different. It's not just the cheating, either. He's distant, has this constant edge of pissed off. He drinks a lot. He's not . . . I don't know how to say it. He's not the guy you're thinking of as Uncle Mark. He's not my dad."

"Do you think he's going to leave? I mean, will they get divorced? The affair's over, right?"

"As far as I know." The word "divorce" rung Julian's body like a bell. It suddenly seemed impossible that he hadn't considered they might split. Why would he think they were immune? Why had he assumed they'd work it out, that his mom would make sure they worked it out? To Thea, he said, "I don't think they'd consider divorce." But inside, he felt the shift.

"But why not tell your dad that you know? Wouldn't that make it easier? Then you could confront him and tell him he's an asshole to his face."

"Yeah, but it would hurt my mom so much to think I knew. She's always, you know . . ." Julian switched to falsetto, "'You and your dad need some one-on-one time!' and 'Tell your dad about your A in Chemistry. He's going to be so proud!' She sells the 'number one dad' thing like a shit used car."

Thea burst out laughing, and Julian leaned into the sound like a sluice of clear warm water. He pictured Thea sitting beside him on the steps; he wanted to pull her close and hold on, to kiss her. It was one a.m. in New Hampshire and ten in California. That divide seemed worse than the space. Come here, he thought, or I'll get in the car right now and come there. But instead he said, "I'll call you before my early class tomorrow."

He could hear her smile. "Can't wait!"

"Me neither. Not for the class, I mean, I can't wait to, you know, talk," and Thea laughed again.

"I know," she said. "I do."

When they hung up, Julian leaned back against the concrete steps, pressing his back into the sharp cold edges. The sound of his parents laughing together at the dining room table echoed through him. How had they lost each other after knowing each other for such a long time? Would he lose Thea after having just found her again? He wanted to believe they could hold on; they *would* hold on. He reached out a hand like it could stretch across the continent.

# BREAKING IN

Travis sat in the porch rocker and watched a brown rabbit zigzag through the long grass of the front lawn. He and Tina bought the white rocking chairs when they'd first moved into the house. Home Depot had rows of them arranged in front of the store right after Easter with a big sign that said "Summer's Coming!" Tina had sat in one and rocked back and forth, looking out over the parking lot. She said that it would be nice on summer nights, that they could watch the lightning bugs and rock on the porch like Grandma and Grandpa. .

Never got "next nor near" to being Grandma and Grandpa, Travis thought, but she wasn't wrong. It had been nice—the porch and the rockers, the lightning bugs, the lawn trimmed and edged and cared for. The lawn. Travis lifted his cap and put his hand through his hair. He'd never have let it look like this.

He reached out with the toe of his boot and rocked the empty chair beside him. He remembered doing that with Emma, rocking her while she blew bubbles with the little purple bottle Tina bought her at the grocery store. Emma was four. That was a year ago, just before it all came apart. He was already a fool, just didn't know it yet. His stomach clenched.

Travis put both hands on his thighs, where the heat of the sun was baking through his jeans. He'd thought maybe Megan might be the answer to it all, but that had turned out wrong too. Thinking of it all made him tired. He knew he should go; he had planned to spray Beacon Middle School before the day was out.

Looking out at the overgrown lawn, Travis missed Tina and Emma, missed his life in that house with a sudden and ferocious pain that tightened like a muscle cramp when he tried to move. He wanted to scream or to sob, but Rita across the street was out on the lawn planting flowers. She'd waved when she saw him come up the drive. Rita had been there a long time, raised her kids in the house. She'd dropped off gift baskets and food when Emma was born.

He checked his watch. The super at Beacon would be waiting. "Let him wait," Travis said out loud, and his voice and his carelessness both surprised him.

Right after starting the business, his father won the contract for the four district public schools, and on afternoons like this one, in July and August, in the muggy heat, they'd go into the empty buildings together with the big tanks of Haunt. They started in the cafeteria. Closed up for months, it smelled like feet, like cheese. Spraying along the tops of the walls, behind the cabinets and shelves for storing the food, the plates, he watched roaches cascade down onto the tile floors, a brown downpour, their legs still wiggling.

The whole building was strange, desks pulled into the halls, piled on top of one another, legs up, and the classrooms emptied to the cinderblock and quiet.

Travis remembered standing in the door of the classroom where he'd sat listening to Mrs. Miller, his seventh-grade teacher. The change from the lively room he knew, with posters and books and furniture, to the empty cold shell in front of him had seemed surprising and sad. Two months later, that September, he was back at school, and he would picture what the school had looked like in July. He would walk down the halls and remember the desks piled along the walls, the cork boards bare, and he would think that, even though it all looked real, it was more pretend than other people knew.

He looked sidelong at the front door of the house. His life there had looked so real, so solid. He'd been everything he knew how to be, a husband and a father. He'd said it to Tina when they'd finally ended it. "What else could I have done? What do you want?" He felt betrayed by the surfaces. Knew now there were things he couldn't see living behind the walls, a sadness he hadn't registered.

TRAVIS GOT UP TO GO. He walked down the cement path toward his truck but instead found himself heading around to the garage and punching in the code. The mower was still where he'd left it when he'd put it away last fall, empty and cleaned in the far corner. It won't take any time at all, he thought, and before he could talk himself out of it, he found the gas can and filled the tank and started. By the time he'd finished the front and gone around to the back, he'd convinced himself he was doing it for Emma, doing it so she could enjoy the lawn, play outside. It was why they'd bought the house in the first place, wasn't it? It was what they'd said. "So the kids would have a place to play." He wondered, not for the first time, if any of this mess would have happened if Tina had been able to get pregnant again.

Travis pushed the mower in around the trees at the far edge of the yard, the sweat pouring down his back and legs, soaking through his jeans. He felt good, watching the tall grass give way to the ordered lines he made, feeling the vibration of the mower up through his hands, lifting his cap and wiping the sweat off his forehead with his bandana. He'd always loved mowing the lawn, the sense it gave him of taking care of things, of taking care of his family. When he finished the front and back, he edged out the walk and the concrete block around the back porch. Then he wrote Tina a note and stuck it in the screen door:

"Stopped to get my mail and noticed you hadn't had a chance to do the lawn. Hope you don't mind. I had some time between jobs. T"

Emma called to say goodnight to him, the way she did every night they were apart. His phone lit up with her picture blowing him a kiss and they went through their ritual greeting: "Hello, my little can of sweet corn!"

"Hello, Daddy, I miss you!" After they said good night, Emma said, "Mommy wants to talk to you."

Tina thanked him for the lawn; she said that she'd kept meaning to get it done or to pay someone to come do it. Travis felt his hands go numb, anger seeping into his arms. Someone else cutting the grass.

"Look," he said, trying to smooth his tone out to something reasonable. "I've always liked doing it and I don't mind . . ."

"Oh Lord, Travis," she said, "I can't ask you to do that." He heard plates clattering in the background and pictured her washing up after supper.

"You're not asking me. I'm offering. Just let me do it until . . . well, for the time being."

She was quiet for a long space and he could hear the silverware clinking and the water running and he could picture everything she was doing, the phone scrunched between her shoulder and her head, the messy bun falling out of her hair, the last of the sun sliding out of the dusty window above the sink, sliding over the little wooden lighthouse they'd gotten in Cape May, over the stupid ceramic frog Emma had picked out for her last birthday. He wished he were standing next to her, drying the dishes and putting them away, hearing about her day. He knew she was looking out the window at the trees. She was thinking. His breath got shallow. What the hell, he thought, what the hell is there to think—

"If you're sure you don't mind . . ."

Travis loosened his grip on the phone, almost elated when she said it. He felt like something crucial had been hanging in the balance.

WHEN HE WALKED BACK in the front door the first time, the smell surprised him. Wood smoke, cigarette smoke, and coffee. He always noticed the smells of the houses he sprayed: cleaning chemicals and soaps or grease or onions, but it was the first time he'd walked into a smell that was his own and not his own anymore. He'd put in the wood stove three years ago and he used to love making fires on winter mornings, getting the logs just right so the fire would burn all day. The smell never left, summer or winter; Tina loved the fires and sat curled in front of them, but complained it got into the curtains, the cushions. Travis liked it. He loved the heft of the logs as he picked them out of the pile, loved figuring how to stack them over the twigs and trash so that they'd burn, so that he could keep the house warm. He even liked the smell of her cigarette smoke though he'd tried to get her to quit since they'd been dating.

"You're a nurse!" he'd said. "How can you smoke?"

She'd just laughed and said that lots of nurses did. "Doctors, too. We're superhuman," she'd laughed, "immune!"

He hadn't meant to break in, though that's what Tina called it later.

It was August, a brutally hot afternoon, one of those days when the sun seemed to sizzle in the sky. He'd finished mowing the lawn and had drunk all the water in the gallon jug, and he was drenched through. When he walked up near the house to fill the jug with the hose, he looked in the window. Seeing that shaded room, the familiar furniture, Emma's beach towel hanging on the banister, it was like seeing a friend you'd heard had died walking down the street toward you. He looked in through the window for a long time, remembered sitting on the green couch with his feet up on that coffee table watching football on autumn Sundays.

Then he remembered that he had his key.

That first time he just walked around the downstairs one time. He didn't touch anything. He stood in the cool air and shivered. He filled the jug at the kitchen sink and Snowy came and threaded through his legs, purring, and he picked her up and scratched her head. When she squirmed, he reluctantly let her jump down, then walked through the rooms downstairs and looked at what was the same and what had changed. Tina had put a vase of silk flowers in the empty spot on the bookshelf where his books had been. Not that there were so many. A couple of hardbacks from the college courses he took before he dropped out, *Everyone's an Author*, and the paperbacks his dad had loved—World War II spy stuff and Hemingway. He thought of them packed in the boxes in the closet at the apartment. He tried to think of the last time he'd been alone in the house before the day he moved out. He'd slept on the couch near the end, and Emma would come down in the morning and snuggle in next to him. Sometimes sleeping with her was the only sleep he'd gotten because he'd spent the night jaw clenched, acid climbing from his stomach to his throat.

One morning, they dropped Emma off with his mom and went for a drive. Travis expected they'd put it right, get back on track. As soon as Emma was squared away and they were back on the highway, Travis smiled at Tina and reached for her hand, but she pulled it away, hung her head.

"It's over," she said.

"The thing with the Tancredi guy?"

"No. No, that's been over. That was over before it ever started. I mean you and me. It's. I just. I can't."

He white-knuckled the wheel, stunned, and didn't look at her. He felt something sharp and burning open inside him like a poisonous flower. He started to say all the things he'd said a thousand times. He forgave her. He loved her. Why the fuck? Then he swallowed it all.

"If that's what you want."

THE NEXT TIME HE WENT in the house, he went upstairs. It was right after Labor Day and the leaves were already turning. The nights getting cooler. Travis mowed, then checked the leaf blower and put the gas can in the truck to fill it up for next time. Then he walked up to the porch and looked around at the blank faces of the neighboring houses before he slipped the key in the lock and slid the door open. He stood for a long time in the quiet entrance, looking up the stairs to where the light spilled down from the window in the bathroom. He watched motes of dust float through the afternoon light. It made him remember sitting in church on Sunday mornings as a boy. The house was quiet like that and cool and still.

He ran a finger on the scratches in the hardwood stairs, from the cat, maybe, or from Emma dragging around her toys. Jesus, those things! Mechanical monsters that had no off-switch or volume control. The pink plastic puppy, the one that scared the shit out of him in the middle of the night, it's eyes randomly lighting up in the dark, its mechanical voice, "Take me for a walk, arf!"

Now he didn't even know all her toys. Now when he came to get Emma, he knocked; he stood in the doorway like an unwelcome guest. That pained him more than he could ever say. Emma opening the door to him, like he was a stranger.

When he got to the top of the stairs, Snowy came out of the bedroom and rolled on her back in front of him, purring when he scratched her belly.

"I missed you, too," he said. "Are you happy to see me?" He scooped her and carried her, cradled like a baby, into Emma's room.

On the floor, in the tangle of Barbies and stuffed animals, were the pajamas she'd worn the night before, the cotton shorts and T-shirt with the princesses on them that, just a few weeks ago, he'd gotten out of her suitcase and tried to dress her in to go to the playground.

"Those are my jammies," she told him, hands on her hips, shaking her head. "You're a silly billy!" He looked at the toy chest he'd built her; Tina had painted it pink, and Emma had covered it with flower stickers. He imagined organizing the room, straightening up the dolls and the toys, throwing the pjs in the laundry basket in the closet, but instead he walked down the hallway and looked at the bathroom. Before Emma was born, he and Tina had put in the blue tile floor themselves on a winter weekend, listening to Lyle Lovett and talking about what to name the baby. If the baby had been a boy, Tina said she liked the name Hunter.

"Hunter," Travis repeated, but he thought, what about Travis? His father was Travis and his grandfather. He always thought they'd name a boy Travis. He couldn't believe Tina didn't get that.

He could still see her, his old T-shirt covering her belly, her face rounder and eyes brighter than they'd ever been, sitting cross-legged and smiling, looking out over the floor they'd just finished.

If she'd gotten pregnant again, would it have been a boy?

HE NUDGED THE DOOR of their bedroom open a little wider with his foot, looked in. Tina had bought a new pink bedspread with yellow flowers and new pillows. On the little shelf that used to hold both their names in wooden letters, only Tina's name remained. She'd taken down the framed picture of the two of them holding Emma right after the christening and replaced it with a more recent picture he'd never seen—her whole family standing on the beach, all wearing blue jeans and white shirts, squinting into the wind, smiling. Tina stood beside her sister holding Emma. Travis felt betrayed all over again, not by the affair, but by the way the world slips, changes when you're not looking.

Just for a moment, he looked at the bed and remembered Tina's body, the curve of her ass in his hands, the warm feel of her curled into him when he woke in the night. Then he thought of all that had happened, of other hands touching her, the doctor she'd slept with, Mark Tancredi. Fuck him. He wondered if she still had the necklace the guy had given her. She'd worn it right in front of Travis, lied, told him she'd bought it herself. His throat tightened. Carefully, he pulled the door back to where it had been.

BY THE FALL, TRAVIS had a routine. Every other week when Tina was at work in the afternoon, he'd stop by and mow the lawn, maybe rake the leaves. As the weather got colder, he pulled up the flower beds and got them ready for winter. Every time he came, he went in the house. The only thing he ever took was water from the tap. The only thing he ever touched was the cat.

Tina told him how much she appreciated his help; sometimes she would pack a Tupperware of his favorite cookies or a loaf of baked bread into Emma's backpack. "Mommy said to say thank you," Emma said, hauling out the little container, handing it over. When Emma went to bed, Travis would throw the cookies away. He couldn't say just why they made him furious, but they did.

Travis began to dread the coming cold. He thought maybe he could offer to shovel when it snowed. He wished he could ask her to let him come over mornings and make a fire, but he knew how strange that sounded.

HALLOWEEN WAS THE LAST Wednesday in October. Jack-o'-lanterns grinned at him from either side of the front door. The grass didn't need cutting really, but Travis raked the leaves and set the mower high and went over the whole lawn one last time to get rid of the thatch. Before he went into the house, he sat on the porch in the white rocker just for a minute. The wind had kicked up and poked cold fingers through the spaces between buttons in his barn coat. The coat was the only clothing of his father's he'd kept because nothing reminded him more of his father or kept his father closer than that coat. Travis wrapped his arms around himself and looked out at the leaves sifting down onto his clean lawn, blowing everywhere he'd just raked.

He rocked himself with one foot and looked out at the lawn, then down at his stained brown work boots. He'd been waking up in the middle of the night wondering which decision it was, which moment—her late-night shifts to make extra money, the anniversary trip he put off to finish a contract, suggesting that maybe they didn't need another child. He shuffled through them now like a deck of cards, lining up the suspects, trying to find the exact time where he'd failed as a husband or father.

HIS MOTHER HAD CALLED that morning to ask about Thanksgiving: would he have Emma? No. Did he want to cook at his apartment or come to the house? The house, of course. He couldn't imagine how depressing it would be to try to have a turkey dinner in his little apartment, his two sauce-pots and the microwave. He wished then that he'd had brothers and sisters the way Tina did, a house full of noise and laughter to look forward to. Tina's family had invited Travis and his mother to join them for Thanksgiving ever since the first year he and Tina started dating. He knew his mother loved cooking with the other women, laughing and drinking wine, the children running in and out wanting glasses of milk or another piece of chocolate.

On the phone that morning, his mother said, "It'll be nice. You'll be home." But it wasn't home. He was supposed to be the one to have the home now, to have someplace to bring her, to have the family and the dinner and the kids. That was what their house had been. *Tina's house*, he thought, *it's Tina's house now.*

ON FRIDAY EVENING, he drove over to the house to pick up Emma for the weekend. Tina opened the door. She still wore her purple scrubs and purple rubber clogs, and she looked tired. The word that came to Travis's mind was "bruised," she looked bruised. She asked him to come in, and he followed her to the kitchen, listening for the sound of Emma somewhere in the house.

Tina sat down at the kitchen table without a word and motioned to the chair across from her. He moved a stack of folded laundry and perched on the edge, his elbows on his knees. Snowy threaded through his feet. On the table in front of him were papers and books, a picture that Emma had drawn, a lopsided blue and pink heart under a sky full of crayon green stars. Travis looked down at the picture and up into Tina's face.

"She's at my sister's. I need to talk to you. I need to . . . I don't know how to begin even."

"Are you okay?" Travis said. "Are you sick?"

She shook her head and looked so sad that Travis's mind skipped, and his stomach hollowed out. "Emma?"

"No, no. Nothing like that. It's you, Travis. It's *you*. What have you . . . You've been breaking in." Travis spread his knees and dropped his head into his hands. "You've been breaking into the house. My house."

He didn't move. He didn't breathe because there was no air. *My house.* As if he'd never lived there.

"I want to know why, Travis. I want to know what's going on."

When he looked up at her, she opened the laptop computer on the table in front of her and turned it around. The shock of seeing himself on the screen brought him to his feet. He froze, not able to turn away. The footage was black and white; he watched himself step through the front door. There was a clock running in the corner, a date. He saw himself take off his cap and he saw his own eyes, strained and sad, looking up the stairs. He remembered that day, the clouds gathering in the windows in the background, and he remembered that it had rained later. He remembered each movement as he watched himself make it, and yet everything about the video looked foreign, as though someone else had been able to imitate him exactly.

"I didn't know you'd put in cameras," he said. "You didn't need to . . . You should have . . . ." He got up and walked to the sink and turned his back to her and to the ghost of himself moving on the screen.

"Explain this to me, Travis. Talk to me."

Travis shook his head and stared out at the trees disappearing into dark beyond the kitchen window, their lines being erased. At the far edge of the woods, he could see the lights of his neighbors' houses. A mist gathered in the swales, and for just a moment it looked to Travis like snow. That would come soon.

His gaze shifted and he saw his own face reflected in the dark window like another screen. He was so much less than he had thought he was, less strong, less solid. On the computer, he heard the other Travis walk down the stairs, his boots loud on the hardwood, leaving. He felt thinned to nothing, as unreal as the video image, the shadow of himself in the kitchen window, poisoned by shame.

Tina said, "Talk to me. Talk. Say something."

Travis dropped his head. His ears roared and every muscle tightened and shook and it took him two breaths to realize he was angry, beyond angry, furious. Tina was still talking, saying something about "Promise me never to—"

"Promise!" He growled the word back to her. "*Promise you?*" In the sink in front of him he saw his black-and-white mug with her lipstick print on the edge. A Father's Day gift from Emma. "World's Best." Suddenly, without meaning to, he was screaming. "What promise could mean anything to someone who . . . someone like you . . . What promise . . ."

He picked it up, but then, as though the irony of the thing scalded, he slammed it down.

The mug hit the edge of the sink and exploded, pieces flying everywhere. The jagged edge of the handle sliced a long, ragged line through his palm.

"Travis!" Tina knocked over the chair as she rose. The cat bolted from under the table.

Then came a moment of amazed quiet. Travis could hear his own breath coming hard, like he'd been running fast and had just stopped. He looked at his hand. The blood blooming up through the gash.

"I never meant . . ." They said it at once.

"I know!" Tina said. "I know! I fucked it all up. I did. It doesn't give you the right to come in here like you—"

"Belong?"

Tina steadied herself on the table. "Travis. You can't do this. You can't be here. I can't go back and undo it. I wish I could but—"

Travis turned toward her and then slid his back down the cabinet, closed his eyes, sat on the floor. His head swam. He felt Tina crouch in front of him, felt her pick up his hand, felt her fingers on his pulse. He opened his eyes. "I'm alright," he said. "I'm not . . . I don't need a nurse."

"You never need anything. You're never hurt. Careful, just let me—" She touched the cut gently, wrapped a dishtowel tight around his palm. She let go of the hand, sat down on the floor beside him, her knees pulled to her chest.

"I never knew until I saw the videos how much you . . . how lost you could be. The pain in your face. I just didn't realize."

"Broken," Travis said, closing his eyes again. She was sitting so close he could smell her lemony soap, hear her breathe. He opened his eyes and tried to focus, stared at a red spot of blood on the sleeve of his father's coat. He tried to find a word for what everything felt. "Alone," he said. "I'm exhausted and alone."

Tina put her hand on the dishtowel that covered his. "Me too," she said. "I've felt . . . It was lonely being with you, Travis. You're always good—so good, so reasonable, happy all the time. Even when I cheated, you barely got mad. You were just like, 'No problem, we'll work it out.' God forgive me, but when I saw the video, I was pissed, yes, but part of me thought, *Jesus! There he is*! I felt like I was seeing you, really seeing you, for the first time."

"No," Travis said, "that isn't me. I can do better, be better. If we could—if we could just try—"

"You don't get it," Tina said. "I'm asking you not to do better. If we did try again—" She pulled her hand back from Travis's and shook her head.

"Say what you want to say. Please."

"We'd have to start again, from square one. Say what we feel, not what we think we should." She looked up at the video looping through again. Travis followed her eyes to the image of himself opening the door and looking up the stairs, something desolate and desperate, something open in his face.

# INTERVENTION

Meera therapy-cleaned. When she was upset, unsettled, or thinking through a diagnosis, she'd get out the vacuum and attack the carpets, the roar of the machine like movable walls of sound surrounding her. In the waiting rooms and medical suites, when things were quiet, she'd sometimes walk around wiping down doorknobs and light switches with an alcohol prep pad until the nurses teased her, called her a germaphobe or a 50s housewife.

Now, she squeaked a wad of paper towels up and down the bathroom mirror, watching her face appearing and disappearing behind her hand. and she wanted to scream at her own reflection. Instead, she thumbed the dark circles under her eyes. *Like beetles*, she thought, her eyes hard and bright, her lips chapped and tense. She pulled in a breath, straightened her blouse, smoothed her hair, and then cursed herself for doing it. Who was going to care what she looked like? If the bathroom mirror was clean?

They'd all arrive in an hour. Mark would be home in two. And then?

Meera kept thinking of the day Julian was born, the tense anticipation, the hope and fear. She'd cleaned that day, too. When the contractions were 15 minutes apart, she'd emptied the silverware drawer to clean, resort, polish. Each time the pain hit, she'd white-knuckle the counter in front of her like a wave was trying to wash her away. As soon as she could breathe again, she'd pick up the next spoon and put her head back down. Mark had told her he was on his way.

"Don't drive fast," she said. "I'm fine."

She'd never told him or anyone how scared she'd been—scared of the pushing and tearing, hemorrhaging, so scared of losing the baby.

But she'd also been scared *of* the baby, the change he would bring with him. She'd seen it in her practice, women whose lives were consumed by motherhood. Some of the mothers would laugh about how their lives changed, say things like "I have no life at all now!" Laugh about going to the gym with crackers in their hair or walking into the grocery store with Snow White stickers on their bellies.

But other women looked shattered, especially the ones who hadn't slept, who were depressed for months, manic, paranoid. Meera knew that Julian would change their lives, knew that all mothers spun the wheel, and no one could predict what would happen or how.

Julian. Her boy. Meera looked at the clock on the stove. Forty-five minutes before Julian would be here. After they'd moved him into the dorm in July, Meera worked long hours to stay out of the empty, quiet house. No terrible music, no boy feet pounding up and down the stairs at all hours, no clouds of cologne in the bathroom. All the things she and Mark had laughed about that she missed so much. This wasn't what she'd imagined Julian's first visit home would look like.

Meera opened the refrigerator and stared into the glare. Did she have enough food? Julian was always hungry. What if the family wanted lunch? Was it even okay to think about food, to offer it? She imagined Googling "recipes for an intervention," and "intervention curry chicken," and she laughed for the first time all morning.

She checked her watch again—forty minutes. She shut the refrigerator and started pacing from room to room, realigning pictures and dusting the frames, the mantle, things she'd already dusted.

He's going to be so angry. The words wove through her careening thoughts. She unspooled a length of paper towels and cleaned the windows on either side of the door, imagining Mark walking through it, walking into the living room and seeing the whole group assembled. His mother in her best blue sari sitting in the corner chair the way she always did, her cup of tea in her lap, her eyes huge and tearful. His father, pacing in front of the fireplace like a caged tiger, cursing under his breath in Italian. Julian sullen in the chair nearest the kitchen, Ron near him. She could see it. Mark would be confused at first maybe, and then the muscle in his jaw would tighten; the vein in his temple would jump. He'd look at her as soon as he realized; he'd blame her. He'd be furious and terrified of losing his medical license. She wondered if he'd turn right around and get back in the car. If he'd run.

But where could he go?

And if he stayed? Oh, the things he'd say, the things he'd accuse her of: "This is your jealousy. You've always been jealous of me!" "You are destroying everything I've ever worked for!" and "My parents!? Julian!? You couldn't have talked to me about this privately first?"

"This is what love looks like." She imagined herself saying it to him, and she believed it. But she knew nothing she said could change his mind. That it was his father all of her hopes were pinned on, his father who would get him in the car and to the detox, who would never take no for an answer.

His parents had taken the ferry over from New Jersey, and Julian had driven down from Dartmouth. Their best friends, Ron and Charmel, would be getting into the car in a few minutes.

In half an hour, they'd be assembled, ready for the confrontation, the fight. The intervention.

Meera looked into the kitchen again, Windex and paper towels at the ready. But she'd already cleaned the white marble counters, the refrigerator, the stove. The room looked back at her expectantly.

TWO WEEKS BEFORE, A FRIDAY, Meera had gotten home from the hospital. She'd just admitted Dori Hughes, a ten-year-old, to ICU in diabetic crisis. They'd almost lost her three times before they could get her stabilized. Dori had struggled with endocrine issues from infancy, so everyone in the hospital knew her, knew the Hughes family. Seeing them go through hell again and not having better answers had devastated Meera and all the specialists they worked with.

Exhausted, starving, defeated, Meera opened the front door and went right to the fridge without flicking on the lights. She'd been eating left-over pad Thai out of the white box when her phone rang, and she saw Julian's name.

"My little boy!" she sang, grateful for the moment of peace and distraction.

But he didn't respond as he usually did with "My mama." Instead, he said, "I have to talk to you, mom." His voice sounded broken.

"Oh, Jules!" An accident? Was he sick? Had something awful happened to one of his friends? "You can tell me," she said, putting down the food.

"It's Dad. Something's wrong."

That sentence stopped her breath. She suddenly knew everything he was about to say. All the things she'd seen but had tried not to see—the mood swings, the lies, the time gaps that made no sense. It was like a heavy fog lifting off her life. She instantly saw the contours of everything that had been there all along. She put one hand to her mouth and whispered, "Yes."

The week before, Mark had driven to Dartmouth at her insistence. She thought he and Julian needed to have some father/son time. She thought one of them should be at his lacrosse game.

"He was supposed to meet me on campus before the tournament," Julian told her. "He got there four hours late and said he'd gotten lost. That's such bullshit."

"He told me he got off on the wrong exit, got a little turned around," Meera said.

"Four hours, Mom! You can't get lost for four hours if you've got a cell phone and a working brain. I can't stop thinking about it, about all the weird shit, all the time he spends in the basement—"

When she calmed Julian down and they hung up, Meera stared at the basement door, deciding. Then she descended the stairs into the cool darkness and went to the spot across from Mark's woodworking bench, to the hidden opening in the white paneled wall that she already knew would be there. When she pushed on the panel, the latch released with the same soft click she'd been hearing and not hearing for weeks.

Inside were plastic crates turned over to make shelves: booze, an envelope of cash, prescription bottles. "Oh," she said, and the shape of their lives, their life together, shifted like a kaleidoscope pattern. She closed her eyes and opened them slowly, as though she might see this new pattern better. "Of course," she said. "Of course. Of course." She picked up two of the prescription bottles—Klonopin and Xanax.

She paced around the basement, taking the same long, slow breaths she told her sick kids to take when they were in pain. She found herself looking at the shelves in the corners, looking under the ping-pong table, like she might find some desperate junkie crouched there, someone who wasn't Mark. She walked across to the workbench against the wall, felt the betrayal of all the expensive tools piled on it. Then she brought the two pill bottles in her fists down hard on the edge of the table, stunned, frightened, furious at the intricacy of the lies, Mark's orchestration of this other self.

NOW, MEERA PUT THE cleaning stuff away under the sink and leaned against the counter and looked across the hallway at the closed basement door. Looking at it filled her with such dread. She hadn't been down there since she'd found the hidden closet, since that Friday night. She'd called Ron before she even left the basement, and he'd immediately suggested the intervention. It had shocked her. "Shouldn't we . . . I don't know . . . try something else? Confront him?"

Ron said that he'd been trying to talk to Mark about it for weeks. "You see what he's taking. We can't mess around with this anymore. If he hurts someone, if he hurts himself—"

They agreed.

She'd been climbing the steps back to the kitchen when Mark called.

"Meera Mine! How are you? I heard about Dori Hughes. Are you okay?"

His voice went through her, and she pushed down the lightning bolt of anger and the wave of disbelief and sat abruptly on the steps. He sounded so normal, so much himself. She fought the desire to tell him what she'd found, what she knew. *You are a lie. Everything about you is a lie.* Instead, she said, "I'm just tired."

"She's going to be fine, you know. Are you beating yourself up for not seeing it?"

Meera lowered her head to her knees. "I am. I am indeed."

These last two weeks, though she berated herself for it. She'd avoided opening the basement like some timid character in an M. Night Shyamalan film, waiting for whatever it was she couldn't face to come creeping up the stairs. It wasn't just the bottles and the pills. Somewhere down there were all the ways their lives were falling apart. She thought of the pictures tacked over the workbench—the simple table Mark said he wanted to make. He said his therapist thought something creative would be the perfect stress reliever. They'd even joked about the basement being his "man cave."

The therapist, the woodworking, all part of the "healing" after the affair. All, *all* a lie. Some "sitcom self" he'd invented for her, and she'd been so sure it was real. Sure, they were on the road to a better marriage. They'd gone on dates again. They'd talked about a second honeymoon. He'd started leaving notes in the backpack she took to work like when they were first together, Post-its that said "I love you, Meerabita," or "Buona Giornata, Cucciola," "You're my heart." He texted her funny gifs and bought her flowers when he went to the grocery store. The thought of it, all of it, turned her stomach.

Scenes from the last few months splintered into shards of glass. Mark slipping the therapist's card into her hand: Dr. Amelia Jensen, specializing in couple's therapy. Mark suggested that maybe they could see her together sometime. That was in the summer—July maybe. They'd been sitting on the back porch with a bottle of wine as the sun went down. She'd noticed then the paler spot on his wrist where his watch would have been, but she hadn't thought more of it. Why hadn't she asked him about it? And where was it now? Would he have sold it, pawned it? A gift from his parents when he graduated medical school, would he actually have done that? She would have said no before, but now she knew he might have.

He'd overdrawn the checking account twice in the last three months and always had some convoluted story about moving money around or the bank making a mistake. The second time, she'd suggested calling the accountant and sitting down with her to take inventory. "Now that Julian's in college," she said, "it would be a good moment to talk about the future, financial planning."

He'd brushed it all aside. "Soon," he said, "sure. When things are less busy." He'd had four glasses of wine that night. Why did she know that? How long had she been counting, noticing without noticing?

And what about the affair? He'd said it was over. She'd told no one, not Charmel, not her sister, Samira, and certainly not Julian.

She assumed Ron knew, though they'd never spoken of it after the day she found out.

A gorgeous Saturday afternoon in May, Mark breezed into the kitchen with his gym bag over his shoulder and said that Ron had just called. They were going to play racquetball, then go out to get a bite. He'd seemed light, relaxed, for the first time in days, and Meera had been relieved.

Mark and Ron had been friends since high school, stayed friends even though Ron went to law school and Mark to med school. Ron had been his best man, Julian's godfather. They got together with Ron and Charmel every other week for dinner. Their daughter, Thea, was almost the same age as Julian.

An hour after Mark left, Meera opened the front door and found Ron with one hand on the doorframe, smiling. She said, "Where's Mark?"

"I stopped by to see if he was—"

Meera felt her mind stutter. "He's with you. Playing racquetball. He's—You called this morning." She looked behind Ron as if her husband might suddenly appear.

"I never called," Ron said. "We had no plans."

They stood silent for a moment, and then Meera remembered herself and said, "Come in! I'm sorry. Come in."

Ron walked into the kitchen and leaned against the counter awkwardly. "Let me call him."

Meera picked up the dishtowel on the counter, folded and refolded it. She kept seeing Mark's back going out the door, the handle of the racquet sticking up from the bag.

Ron waited as the machine picked up, shook his head. "I'm at your house," Ron said. "I think there's been a misunderstanding." When he left, he'd only said, "We'll sort this out," but he looked at Meera with great kindness.

MARK CAME THROUGH THE DOOR two hours later, already a wreck. He cried so hard when he told her, she thought he might have a seizure. Some nurse he worked with. Married. The hospital soap opera cliché. His hands shook. Later she heard him vomiting in the bathroom. At the time, she'd believed the physical symptoms were evidence of how sorry he was, how lost. Now she wondered if he'd been in withdrawal.

MEERA WENT UPSTAIRS to their room, rooted through the drawer in her bureau, found the clip she was looking for, and put up her hair. She got a damp face towel out of the laundry and dusted the windowsills, then looked out the bedroom window at the driveway, leaned her forehead on the cool glass. She tried to breathe, but her lungs were steel and couldn't absorb air.

In ten minutes, they'd all arrive. They'd park around the corner so Mark wouldn't see the cars. They'd sit in the living room and talk reasonably with someone who couldn't be reasoned with. She thought she should go downstairs and put on a pot of coffee, get the kettle ready for tea, but she didn't move. She felt her own pulse throbbing like a clock in her chest and throat.

Her mind jumped between the two outcomes. Maybe this would be the best thing that could happen. Mark would accept the diagnosis. He'd recover. They'd piece their lives back together a little at a time—meetings, rehab visits, doctor's appointments—until they'd found the far shore.

Or, Mark would deny, resent, refuse to go anywhere, and she would turn him into the board. It would end their marriage. She knew that, but she had no idea what would come after that. Meera felt her stomach hollow out like she was looking down from a high cliff. She stared at the bright red leaves of the dogwood tree in the front yard. She and Mark had planted it with Julian when the boy was three. She picked up the cloth and looked around the room. She thought, "I should go down and . . ."

But there was nothing left to do. She watched as the breeze lifted the leaves of the dogwood and shook the tops of the tall trees across the street. Then she felt for the first time in days something like peace. People she loved would be there in minutes, and they would bring into the light what had been growing in darkness. It might tear them all apart or be fresh hope, but whatever was coming, like the breeze, was already on the way.

# ASHES

My sister-in-law believes in ghosts, believes that almost everyone really is a good person deep down, believes that all children can learn if they're taught right. Sylvie's a first-grade teacher, the kind who keeps all the stupid, little gifts the kids give her—the plaque that says "Best Teacher Ever" and the plastic apple mounted on a stack of plastic books that says "Teacher Trophy." All of it. The shit they draw for her, even the cards they made for her when my brother died.

It's weird to think my brother has been gone for more than a year. Sometimes I still forget and think I'll call him. Sometimes it seems like a thing I've always known, always lived with.

When I found out I was pregnant, one of my first thoughts was that the universe had made a mistake: this should be Sylvie and Jeff's child. I should've been the one we buried. But I don't mean that. I know the universe doesn't care. Sylvie says everything happens for a reason, but I don't believe that either.

Time fools you. I was three months pregnant before I found out. Twelve weeks.

I want the baby in a way I didn't know I could want anything, with every cell of my body. I need to tell my mother. I need to tell my boss, of course. I need to tell Sylvie.

And Brian. I know Brian will freak. Absolutely. He was Jeff's best friend, and we slept together just twice. Once after the funeral, and once four months ago, on the anniversary of Jeff's death. That's the start of all this in some ways, but really it goes back way longer. I've always had a crush on him, ever since we were teenagers, and I would hang out with him and Jeff. We'd go to the movies sometimes and bars when we got old enough. I just tagged along, but Brian never made me feel like that. We both loved science and nature, and we'd have these great conversations about pollinators or wetland ecosystems until Jeff couldn't take it anymore. He'd complain that he'd spent the whole day studying Organic Chem or Vertebrate Morphology and could we shut up already about all that.

Brian never felt anything like a crush on me, God knows. Not then, not now. He likes toenail polish and heels, wasp waists, some sort of blonde ballerina in a power suit. That's his search image. We're friends. Not that we hang out all the time or anything, but we call each other pretty much every week and text each other. Sometimes he stops in if he's passing by. Sometimes we have breakfast at the diner on a Saturday. We haven't seen each other in the last four months. We've been talking on the phone, texting, but sleeping together the second time . . . it didn't work like I'd imagined, hoped. No curtain lifted so that he saw me differently. No lightning bolts. We didn't even really talk about it this time. He doubled down on the friendly tone after but kept his distance.

So, I keep trying to imagine how I'm going to tell him, how it's going to go. Maybe a text "BTW I'm pregnant with your baby. We should maybe talk." Not funny. He's going to want to know what I want from him. Nothing is the answer to that. Nothing. Not that I'd say no if he offered.

And then there's Sylvie. She's going to be even harder to tell than Brian. I know this is going to hurt her, unearth all the regrets, the grief. She'd wanted kids with Jeff, but Jeff pulled the scientist crap on her—too many people, humanity is a slime mold, yadda yadda. She had no defense against it. They'd made a sort of "no kids" pre-nup, and he called her on it, and she wasn't the kind of person who was going to tell him, like I would have, that he was full of shit and just afraid to be a father because our father left. Besides, even with all the stuff I learned in ecology classes, I knew one kid more or less didn't matter. Sometimes I imagine how different it would have been for her, for me too, if there'd been a little more Jeff left in the world.

But maybe that's my full-of-shit thinking. Would having someone with Jeff's genes who wasn't Jeff make the world better? Having one more person who missed him?

I decided to tell Denny, my boss at Chick's Farm and Feed Supply, first. He was the easiest. Denny's about sixty with a red face and big gut that hangs over his jeans. He looks like the farmer his dad was before his dad started Chicks, named it for his mom. Denny's whole family is Lutheran and Bible study and dead Jesuses hanging all over, so a single, pregnant woman shuffling around the store will definitely be a problem. But he likes me enough to do the "hate the sin and love the sinner" dodge, and he'll talk his father around, too, though his father is mostly retired now and just comes in the store to meddle and drive Denny crazy.

Besides I do everything—the books, some inventory, sales. Two years ago, I suggested that Chicks move into pet food and dog grooming. People with horses and cows all have dogs and cats, dead certain. And they'll spend a surprising amount of money on Fido. That's been pulling in a fortune, so pregnant with a bastard child or not, my guess is he won't fire me.

My mother still thinks it's a damn shame that someone with a college education—a degree in ecology and wildlife management—should be working in a feed store. When I first got the job, she used to shake her head and roll her eyes, and if I told her I liked what I did, she'd change the subject, figure out a way to get off the phone. She thinks I work in a feed store because I'm fat, and it's her fault I'm fat because she let me eat too many Ding Dongs when I was a kid, and if I just lost like fifty pounds, I'd magically transform into a Disney Princess and get the right job and the right man and the right life. When I told Sylvie all that, so we could have a laugh together, she was quiet instead and then she said, "You might feel more confident, you know. It might help."

Well, goddamn.

I'm not lacking confidence. I do the things I want. And I'm in better shape than anyone gives me credit for. I ride horses; I hike. I'm not scared of anything.

Except I'm scared right now. I'm scared to have this baby. I wake up at night in a cold sweat with my heart pounding out of my chest.

And, I'm scared about Brian. I told a lie to get him to sleep with me the second time, and I'm scared, terrified really, that now that I'm pregnant the lie will come out. It was a stupid lie, a big one. I just didn't think he'd ever take the chance of getting together with me in a date kind of way if I didn't give him some good reason. The one-year anniversary of Jeff's death was part of a good reason, but I didn't think it was enough. He could have blown that off. I told him I'd saved some of Jeff's ashes for the two of us to scatter in Cape Henlopen State Park, to give Jeff "back to the ocean." I heard Sylvie's voice in my head even as I said it. It didn't sound like me at all, but he didn't call me on it. He agreed, said it would be the perfect thing to do.

Right before I went to meet him at the park, I threw some chicken bones and hair from the pet groomers and sticks and paper into the incinerator at work, and I scooped the ashes into a box. I threw that box into the backseat with a bottle of Jameson, his favorite, and off I went. And, God help me, I knew exactly what I was doing.

Except about getting pregnant. I swear I didn't plan that part.

THE FIRST TIME Brian and I got together was right after Jeff's funeral. The whole family went to lunch in this stuffy dining room restaurant, and after, the two of us snuck off to one of the bars we used to go to with Jeff when we were all in our twenties. I remembered the smell as soon as we walked it—beer and chemical cleaner—the awful sticky floor and wobbly tables.

"Was it always this much of a dive?" Brian laughed. "Jesus." He gets this single dimple on his left cheek when he laughs or smiles big.

Then we drank beer and cried. Brian got pretty drunk. I pretended to be drunker than I was. We went back to my place.

I didn't expect it all to mean so much to me. He fell asleep and I lay curled behind him touching his back and sort of marveling at the bones of his spine, the muscles extending from them like wings. I had half a thought that maybe this was the beginning of something.

The next morning, though, he couldn't meet my eyes.

That was a year ago, and we kept it all firmly in the friend zone ever since. But that one night grew in my mind and cast a long shadow. I wanted another chance. More than anything I've ever wanted, I wanted another chance, more time with him, maybe to sleep with him again. I started to think about how I could do it all differently, say things so he could see me differently, so we could connect.

It wasn't like he'd found the love of his life in the meantime. He was still single and so was I, and I just thought, maybe there was a reason why. So, I planned it, right down to suggesting that we have a couple of shots at the overlook and toast to Jeff. I planned it, but I never thought—

He still talks to Sylvie all the time, meets her for coffee, checks in. He talks to my mother, too. I can imagine fifty ways for it to come out that I asked him to the park to throw Jeff into the ocean and my mother and Sylvie howling that we'd scattered every ash two weeks after Jeff died. I can imagine the looks on all their faces when they realize what the hell I've done. How I've done it.

But I never meant to get pregnant, and I wasn't being careless. I had my diaphragm in, I swear to God I did. When I told my ob-gyn that I was wearing it, he asked if I'd been refitted in the last two years—which of course, I hadn't—and then he asked if I'd gained any weight. I raised my head as best I could and looked him square in the eye over the drape across my legs. I asked him how in the hell that could make a difference.

"They're like anything you wear," he said. "They don't fit if you lose or gain too much weight."

Well, fuck.

PEOPLE SURPRISE YOU. I told Denny I was pregnant Monday morning while we were looking over the feed inventory. He'd just gotten in, and his cheeks were still bright red from the cold, and he had his ski hat on. I took the paper from his hands real gentle and said the sentence I'd been working on while I was lying awake in bed all night. "Denny, I have something serious to tell you, and I'm hoping it doesn't change the way you feel about me as an employee or a person."

How's *that* for a momentous opener? He looked pretty much how I thought he would, immediately on guard. But when I told him, he put his hand on my arm and then just pulled me into a hug, our bellies mushed together. He looked at me so concerned. He said, "You alright? Is everything going to be okay? You been to a doctor? Course you've been to a doctor. Are you ... single? Do you know who—course you know. Will you be a single mom? Who'll help you?"

It all came out in a torrent, but the look on his face was so parental and concerned and I hadn't expected that at all. It made me believe the whole thing would turn out better than I thought.

I went to the ladies right then and called Brian. When he didn't pick up, I left a message on the machine. I'd practiced that, too, the night before. I tried all kinds of variations of it:

"Hi, Brian"

"Hello, Brian"

"Brian, it's Regina"

"Brian, I need you to call me as soon as you get this."

I ended up going with something less dire. "Hi, Brian. It's Regina. Can you give me a call back? Thanks." I struggled to make my voice steady and normal.

I tried to think of where he'd want to be when I told him this. Part of me wanted to tell him in public—at the diner, maybe, or in one of the coffee shops he always took women to so they wouldn't cry too much when he broke up with them. But telling him in public felt too mean. He should be able to yell at me if he wanted to, to curse me. I really hoped he wouldn't though. I wasn't sure I'd be able to keep myself from sobbing if he did that, and I hated that picture: him freaking out and me ugly crying in the face of it. No matter what setting I put that in, it didn't work.

All day I waited for my phone to buzz in my pocket, and nothing. All day I tried to forget about it and just wait, but it was like a loose tooth you can't stop wiggling. I'd take my phone out and look at it and put it back, then wait on a customer or two, then take it out again. I was grateful to be at work because it would have been much worse at home.

Once when I took out my phone, Denny looked at me sympathetically and said, "Are you waiting for a call from the doctor?"

I nodded.

When I got off work and still hadn't heard from Brian, I drove by the lab. His car was there in the parking lot, so I drove by again, and then again. *Stop stalking him*, I told myself. You're not getting any more pregnant. You'll tell him when you tell him. Go home.

But I couldn't face going home, and I didn't know what to do, so I stopped by Café a Go Go. I was just about to order my usual Americano with two shots of espresso when I heard my mother's voice in my head. "That's a lot of caffeine for the baby." Christ. I hadn't even told her yet and she was already at me. I ordered an herbal tea instead and started for the door.

Then Brian walked in.

He was looking down at his phone, his hands red from the cold, and he looked up and broke into a wide grin. "I was texting you back just this minute! Sorry. Today was crazy. I kept meaning to . . ."

He was thinner, more drawn somehow than four months ago. I didn't expect what seeing him for the first time in months would do to me, didn't expect it at all. Suddenly it was real. There was a life inside me that belonged to Brian, too. Whatever happened next, everything would change for both of us always. The full realization almost doubled me over.

"Regina?" Brian said. "Are you . . .? Is everything okay?"

I tried to smile and couldn't. "I need to talk to you," I whispered.

He put his hand under my elbow. "Sit down," he said. "I'll get a coffee."

"Not here!" It came out so much more panicked than I meant it to, and I tried to cover it with a fake laugh that ended up sounding maniacal. Breathe, for Christ's sake! I told myself. Brian stood in front of me with his hands at his side looking down at the chair I was refusing to sit in. "Let's take a walk," I said.

"It's cold, and it's going to rain."

"I don't mind. It won't rain hard."

Brian looked at me quizzically and nodded. "Do you mind if I get some coffee?"

"No," I said. "No, of course. Go right ahead."

I stood by the door and watched him shift his weight from foot to foot. He looked back at me once, a quick, worried glance, then pulled his wallet from his back pocket and paid.

I held the hot cup of tea tight to my chest because I was suddenly shaking. I'm never cold, but I was freezing.

We walked in silence for a half a block. The January rain a silver mist that frosted the warm windows of stores and that I blinked out of my eyelashes. The gray sky closed down over us. We were alone on the sidewalk, and the cars that drove by turned on their lights and wipers.

Finally, Brian said, "Is it your mom? Sylvie? What's wrong? Something's wrong."

"No, no. Nothing like that. It's me. I don't know where to begin."

Brian turned and stepped in front of me and we stood face-to-face. I wanted to grab him and hold him, to burrow my head into his chest, so I took a step back.

"What's happened? Something. Are you sick? Don't tell me you're sick!" He stepped in again and lifted his fingers to barely touch my cheek. "You're pale," he said.

He dropped his hand, and I immediately wished he would touch me like that again. Even when we'd made love, he hadn't touched me that gently. His eyes were full of concern, dread almost, and it shocked me. He was scared to lose me, and I thought of Jeff, and something just broke inside.

"They weren't Jeff's ashes!" The blood rushed to my head and made me dizzy.

Brian looked at me like he thought I might be having a stroke. "What?" he said. "What do you mean they weren't . . . what?"

"The ashes we scattered in the park together. They weren't Jeff's ashes." *Nice, I thought. Nice job, Regina.*

"Whose ashes were they?"

"I'm pregnant," I said.

He started to say "What" but it came out as just a "wh-"

"They weren't anyone's ashes. They were just ashes because I thought—I wanted to sleep with you, to sleep with you again, and I thought if I could, you know, recreate something like the first time, and maybe this time, you'd see me differently, like me better, but you didn't. And that's fine. That's fine. Or it would be fine, except now I'm pregnant, and—" I finally drew a breath. "Oh, Jesus," I whispered. "Let me start again."

He looked down at my middle and instinctively I covered my belly with my arm.

"No one has to know but you and me. No one. I'm not asking you for anything at all. I've got this. I just thought you should know because, because I didn't want to lie. I mean, I lied about the ashes part, but I didn't want to . . ."

He looked over my shoulder and blinked like he was trying to bring something into focus that was still in the far distance. Then his eyes snapped back to mine. "You wanted to have my baby?" He said it like the words were in another language he had just learned.

"No!"

A man across the street turned his head.

"No," I said it again, searching around for some reasonable volume, tone, but it all came out louder and more desperate than I meant. "No, you've got to understand that. I never wanted to get pregnant. I didn't plan this at all, in any way, ever. I just, I wanted to sleep with you." It sounded so high school, so pathetic, but everything I could think of to say sounded that way. "I . . . like you. I've always really liked you. That's why—the ashes, the bottle, all of that."

Now it was Brian who looked like he needed to sit down, and I tried to steer him toward one of the white benches that lined the sidewalk on the beach block, but he shook off my hand.

"Why didn't you just ask me if you wanted to sleep with me?"

"Would you have done it if I'd just *asked*?"

He opened his mouth and then shut it. He picked up the pace, his long legs gobbling the sidewalk in big bites. I couldn't keep up, especially in the work boots.

I stopped. He didn't notice I wasn't beside him. So, I thought, so, this is how it's going to be. I called after him, "If you want to run, you can. Just go. I'm not asking anything from you. Not money. Not a relationship. Nothing."

He stopped then and walked back the half block. He looked at me like he'd never seen me before. "Is it a boy or a girl?" He said it like a challenge. "What? What does it fucking matter? It's a baby." I stretched myself tall and stepped closer to him, challenged back.

Then he caught me by the shoulders. "It doesn't fucking matter, but it's my baby, so is my baby a boy or a girl?"

*My baby.* The words buzzed in my brain. I grabbed his arms. "I don't know. I won't know until next month when they do the ultrasound."

He dropped his arms and started to laugh, a quiet laugh, but a real one, not bitter or hurt, just a little crazy.

"What?" I said. "What's funny?"

"I'm just thinking of Jeff. How hard would Jeff have laughed if he could have seen us scattering those ashes that weren't him? Jesus, he would never stop making fun of us. Giving him back to the ocean. What total crap."

And then I was laughing too. "He would hate that I'm pregnant. Bringing someone else into this—"

"Catastrophically crowded world." We both said it at once.

Brian said, "He *did* have his soap boxes."

I pictured Jeff sitting at the kitchen table when we were in college, a book open in front of him, a cup of coffee. I was leaning against the counter, and he was laughing at something I said, the yellow of the overhead lamp making a circle of light around him.

"He would be furious at me," I said again, and knowing that made me feel so terribly alone.

We started to walk again, and the rain came down harder and started to freeze. I was shocked that Brian was still beside me, and I looked at him sidelong like he might bolt at any minute.

People coming out of stores popped umbrellas and walked fast. My feet were dry in the work boots, but my jeans were soaked. I looked down at Brian's sneakers and realized that he must be cold. "I thought you would be furious, too," I said.

"If he'd lived just a little longer," Brian said, and then he stopped and started again, "If any part of Jeff exists somewhere in the universe—and what the hell do I know about the universe—no part of him is furious at you. I'm not either. I don't know why. I guess I should be, but I think maybe . . . this is good. This is what I need."

Around us the world dissolved into water, the hush of frozen rain on the pavement, hiss of passing cars, the rise and fall of the ocean behind us. I thought of the dark and particular ocean at my own center, our baby rising and falling on the waves of my breath.

# PAIN

## I.

She came into the bank every other Friday afternoon. The first time I waited on her, she passed the check and the deposit slip across the counter to me, but I didn't really notice her face. I looked at her hands. They were long and fine, her fingernails short and unpolished and dotted with paint of all different colors. No rings. It took me more than a month before I got up the courage to ask her what she did that her hands were always constellations of color or smudged with clay like gray clouds, and that's when we started talking.

I thought she might teach pre-school. I had done that for a while, years ago, after the divorce, before I found the teller job. But she looked too edgy, too cool to be a teacher. She might have painted furniture or done something like that, but I was almost sure she was an artist. She looked like an artist—I think that was part of what attracted me. She wore jeans with spikey roses embroidered above the hip pocket, reading glasses in odd colors, lavender or bright green. She was like no one else who came into the bank, like no one else I'd ever known.

## II.

On Fridays, I'd watch out for her if I was working the drive-through window, wait for her green pick-up to pull into the parking lot, wonder what music she was listening to, what she was thinking when she sometimes sat out there for a few minutes, her head down, resting on the steering wheel. When she came through the door, none of what she must have been feeling was in her face, and I wanted to ask her if everything was okay.

I would try to switch with whoever was working the counter so I could talk to her. I wanted to say, "I feel that way sometimes, but I never let myself put my head down, even for a second." Sometimes I imagined saying that, how she might reach for my hand. I knew I'd never do it.

When she first used my name—Rita—I was flustered, and then she pointed at my name tag, and we laughed. "Jo," she said, reaching out her beautiful, callused hand. "I'm Jo."

That afternoon, after Jo left, I stood behind the counter watching her walk across the parking lot, and then I went to the ladies' room, ran the tap as cold as I could get it and splashed my face. I looked sternly into my own plain brown eyes and silently ordered myself to stop whatever this was I was doing.

## III.

I told myself it was grief. My son died over a year ago in a bicycle accident, thirty-five-years-old. No one dies at thirty-five. That was the refrain my brain played over and over during those months. No one dies at thirty-five. Like the universe might realize the mistake and give him back.

I kept trying to be strong for Sylvie, for Regina. But nothing made any sense that spring. The light was wrong. I couldn't sleep for more than an hour at a time, and I'd wake up already crying.

## IV.

I told myself it was loneliness. I'd been alone since Jeff and Regina were toddlers, decades, a lifetime. Ever since that

August morning when I woke up to find the note their father left propped by the coffee maker, the morning I cried as much in relief as sadness. As much about what I would do for a car, as what I would do without him.

All these years later, driving to work, I took deep breaths at the stop lights and looked at the fall colors creeping into the trees along the avenue. I tried to reason with myself—this attraction to Jo was a symptom. I was confused. I was alone.

I was not gay. That's what I told myself. I'd never been gay before; you can't just suddenly come down with it like a cold. Clearly. I probably liked her because she seemed caring, because she was an artist and I'd never known an artist before. I knew they were everything I wasn't—brave, creative, passionate. And everything I wasn't was everything I needed to be. How would I cope with Jeff's death, help Sylvie and Regina, put my life back together, or maybe even put together a life for the first time? How could I do those things without courage and creativity?

Jeff's death had torn something open—not in me, but in the world. It didn't feel at all like other people said it did. When I went to the grief group at the hospital, we sat in a circle and people said they kept their feelings "bottled up" or they felt like they would suddenly "explode."

I felt, instead, like I'd been living in a walled garden. Jeff's death had blown away the walls and I stood for the first time, open to the horizon. Stunned, disoriented, terrified.

V.

Jo seemed to be walking toward me from a long way off. She might step over one of those crumbled walls and touch me. But that also felt insane. Some voice inside kept repeating, *You are fifty-four-years-old, and you have never felt this way before about a woman, any woman.*

But then I would think this, *You are fifty-four-years-old and you have never felt this way before. Ever.* And, cliché as it was, I couldn't deny it was true. I had never known how to want the relationships that other people seemed to. I'd never had passion. My mother used to call me a wallflower, and I guess I was. Shy and bookish, I'd never pursued anyone, never thought I'd be married.

I'd met Martin on a blind date because a friend of mine from the community college liked his brother. She set it up that the four of us would go bowling. Such a fiasco! The ball was so heavy I thought my fingers would break just lifting it. Martin laughed easily. He had a lopsided grin, thick blond hair, and a quiet demeanor that everyone, including me, mistook at first for shyness, though it was something much deeper.

We shared that something, I think. A basic inability to face our own emotions. Maybe that's what attracted us to each other. We had, right from the start, an unspoken agreement about how much we would ever force the other to feel, to say.

The night we got engaged, I said to Martin, "I just never thought anyone would marry me." His eyes got a faraway look, and he reached across the car seat and grabbed my head and held me awkwardly against his chest.

We were so young. Since then I've wondered who he thought I was that I didn't turn out to be.

## VI.

Right before Christmas, Jo walked away from my window and then came back and asked if I wanted to go for coffee.

## VII.

I got to the coffee shop a full hour early because I was so nervous and because I didn't want her to see me walk in. In the bank, I stood still and she walked toward me, that was the way it had always been, and I didn't understand why, but that seemed right. I brought a journal article with me. After Jeff died, I'd started reading self-help books, medical journals, anything I could find about grief or pain.

I had to keep myself from scanning for Jo, and kept pulling my eyes down to the page. She will not be here for a good long while yet, I told myself. I read the first sentence of the abstract: "Pain of any origin comprises an individual's life. The prevention and management of pain is an important aspect of health care. Psychological factors play a key role in both onset and progress of any pain disorder."

My eyes drifted to the side of the page: K. Hanoch Kumar, from a dental college in Maharashtra, India, July 2000.

The coffee shop wasn't crowded, and I raised my eyes every time the bell on the door jingled. Then I forced them down to the page again. "The chore of medicine is to preserve and restore patient's health and to minimize their suffering. To achieve these goals, intellection about pain is a must because pain is universally understood as a pointer of disease, and it brings the patient to the physician recognition."

The strange, stilted prose made me see the man somehow. It felt like he was working hard to say something about how pain could be good, about how pain could make someone visible, real. I imagined him standing at a tea stall outside the dental college, sweating in the heat and dust.

Then Jo suddenly sat down at the table and my heart took off. Where had she come from? I grabbed the article, flustered, and I said, "Oh, oh, here you are, already, here you are!" and I tried to shove the xeroxed papers back into my bag, but she slapped them still with one hand and read the title and laughed. "'The Description and Management of Pain'? Should I take this personally?"

That was our beginning. She'd tease me about that article on and off whenever she did something that she knew I'd be mad at, something that frustrated me. She'd look at me over her glasses and say, "The Description and Management of Pain," and as often as not, I'd laugh helplessly.

## VIII.

When the pain first came, she'd stretch out on the couch or put her head on the table in the kitchen; we still went to the grocery and played with the dog. It was before she'd retired. By the time we met, she'd already done almost thirty years of teaching painting, drawing, ceramics, sculpture. She'd been a teacher after all—art, of course! Thirty years of fourteen-year-olds who became eighteen-year-olds before her eyes. Thirty years of lopsided roses with the colors mixed wrong, clay pots that broke in the kiln. We dreamed of going to Barcelona, to Paris, to Seville. She'd always wanted to go to Seville. Her favorite painters, Murillo and Velazquez, were born there, and she thought the quality of light in their paintings was the light of the city they grew up in.

We looked at the brochures, dreamed of time. She dreamed of coming home from travel to spend whole days painting in the plein air, painting late at night in her studio, the way she had when she was young. Painting and painting with no other obligation, no sense of time.

## IX.

When Jo was eighteen, studying at the Philadelphia College of Art, she'd wander around the city and imagine which galleries would feature her work. She'd dream about a show at the museum, a retrospective. In those dreams, she had her same young face with a shock of white hair, and critics would ask her about the different periods of her long career like she was Georgia O'Keefe or Helen Frankenthaler. When she told me about those dreams, she'd laugh quietly at herself. We'd laugh together about what it was like to have been so young.

## X.

"Pain is whatever the experiencing person says it does."

I found the xeroxed copy of the article in a box filled with miscellaneous papers when we were clearing out rooms so that Jo could move in. I showed it to her, and we laughed. "The Description and Management of Pain." I held it over the pile of trash, but I couldn't drop it. I reread parts. "Pain is whatever the experiencing person says it does." The most unhelpful definition ever!

This was before the doctors and procedures, before I'd watch Jo's face go ashen as she tried to keep making breakfast, before she'd crumple into the chair in the kitchen, and I'd find myself saying, "Is it burning or crushing? Does it feel like a headache?"

"It feels like fire. Like an electrical charge shooting through my jaw, across my forehead, behind my eye."

## XI.

Later, her pain arrived without warning, like a sound, and her arms and legs convulsed like her body believed it could run from itself. When it would leave, she'd sit as still as she could, her body vibrating like a rung bell, before she stood to pick up the brush again. I'd leave the studio then and make her a cup of tea.

Now, near the end, the only ghost, the only living thing left, is the pain. It has hollowed her to a howling silence. I see her, but she is not there.

In the image the doctor showed us, the tumor looked like a bush, like the azaleas I planted in the front yard, and the nerve that the tumor was pressing on looked like the roots of the bush, running across the side of her face, above and below her mouth, under her eye, over her forehead. "Trigeminal," the doctor called it.

## XII.

After that appointment, we came home and stretched out together in the bed, exhausted. I rolled to face her and traced a finger across her cheek where the roots ran. I imagined the pain rising like small fish to meet my touch.

Now, I sit beside her hospital bed every day, sometimes crying, sometimes just talking to her about nothing—about the azaleas or Gaudi's Cathedral, or remembering when we met. I think of her hands covered with paint and clay reaching across the counter at the bank, and I touch the veins that run from her knuckles to her wrist. I pick up her hand and hold it against my face. She doesn't feel me do it, can't hear.

I wait for the pain to say what it will do.

## XIII.

"In Greek word, pain means penalty."

That's the wonderful, awkward, ungrammatical sentence that I will always remember, the one I was reading just as Jo walked in the coffee shop all those afternoons ago. Back then, I thought only about Jeff. I connected "penalty" to his pain and thought it unfair. What had he done to suffer so much? It was only later that I thought about my own grief, about Sylvie and Regina, about Brian. So much pain.

The sentence comes back to me as I watch the nurse come in and switch out the IV bag, press the place where the needle goes into the vein. I scour Jo's face looking to see any tension, reaction, but Jo doesn't wince. Her face looks foreign, hers and not hers at all. I feel bereft. Pain is the penalty for loving anyone, for being loved, for living.

# SOMEONE NEW

The trip had been a plan born of desperation and grief. Sylvie could see that now. After the first anniversary of Jeff's death, she'd been expecting things would begin to get better. That was the way it had always been before—with her mom's death, her dad's. The first year was the toughest; you went through all the "firsts," and then gradually, as the days and weeks passed, the pain softened. It wasn't that you forgot, but the remembering got easier.

Then Regina.

She and Brian were having a baby. *She and Brian.* Sylvie couldn't process it at first. "You're . . . ? How did . . . ? Are you . . ." Sylvie leaned her weight onto the counter behind her.

"I know this sounds crazy," Regina said, lifting her hands from the kitchen table. "Believe me! No one was expecting this, least of all me. No, least of all Brian. I know, too, that maybe it isn't the easiest thing for you to hear. I've been trying to figure out how to tell you."

It was a Saturday morning. Regina had stopped in with doughnuts. They'd been chatting about nothing when Sylvie got up to pour a cup of tea, and Regina said, "I have something I need to tell you."

Now Regina sat with Bowtie's head in her lap scratching his ears. The mug in Sylvie's hands suddenly felt like the heaviest thing she'd ever lifted. A wave of anger and betrayal swept over her. She thought, *Stop touching my dog. I want you out of my house*, but she knew that was crazy.

"Sylvie?" Regina said. "Are you okay? I'll understand if you're really upset or mad. I get it."

With an effort, Sylvie put the mug down and crossed the room. "I'm so happy for you both. I'm happy." She hugged Regina hard and hated that the tears that came weren't the joy and surprise Regina took them for, but a dark bitterness and burning.

A WEEK LATER, SYLVIE walked down the beach with Tina and tried to explain why Regina's pregnancy had derailed her, sent her spiraling into a grief she hadn't felt before.

Sylvie had met Travis and Tina at the first grade meet-and-greet last autumn. Travis shook her hand and said, "We know your . . . that is . . . your ex-mother-in-law lives across the street. Not ex. I don't mean—"

Tina commandeered the conversation so gently, told Sylvie she had been there with Jeff in the ER, that she was so sorry for her loss.

"I don't remember you from that night," Sylvie apologized.

"Oh, no, no, of course! How could you have?"

Emma came and stood beside them. "Daddy lives in our house again," she said, and Travis grabbed her hand and said, "That's true."

As Tina and Sylvie walked, the March sky clouded over, and the wind blew cold and constant off the Atlantic. Regina was five months pregnant and beginning to show. Every time Sylvie saw her, she felt a storm of emotions—anger, grief, bitterness, and a loss she couldn't understand. This loss, even more than Jeff's death, had packed cotton between Sylvie and the world around her. Food was tasteless, colors dull, nothing was funny, or sad even. Nothing touched her. She had stopped crying, that was true, but she'd also stopped laughing. She was cold to her bones. Frozen all the way through.

She told Tina that ever since Regina announced the pregnancy, it was everything Sylvie could do to get herself out the door mornings. Sometimes it was more than she could do, and she called in sick and hated herself for it. Then she would spend the day wrapped in a blanket and watching television—*Wheel of Fortune*, infomercials for exercise equipment—anything that came on. It didn't matter.

She told Tina she was worried she would be frozen this way forever. "This can't be the rest of my life," she said. "I can't live if this is the rest of my life."

"Look, why don't you take a trip once the school year ends? Get out of Dodge for a while. You need a break is all, a change, a way to jump start the next part of your life."

That was when she'd first thought seriously about Conor's message. About the email he'd sent a few months before. "If you ever want to come to Dublin . . ." She'd never traveled anywhere alone. The thought scared her and thrilled her.

SHE'D GOTTEN THE FIRST card from Conor right after Jeff's death. He apologized for not being able to make it over for the funeral and he'd talked about the good times he and Jeff had as kids when Jeff's parents had stayed for weeks on the family's farm in Kilkenny. Jeff had often talked about the Irish cousins, mimicking their accents, telling stories about moving the cows from field to field or riding the tractor into town. The smell of cut grass on summer nights took him back to the hay barn in Mullivanat. The sound of horses' hoofs on a deserted country road. Sylvie had never had the chance to meet them, but Jeff had kept in touch with Conor and his wife, Róisín, first by letter and then email and later Facebook. He'd even flown over the year before Jeff and Sylvie were married to stand as godfather for their oldest daughter, Maeve.

Maeve had come to the airport with her father and Sean to meet Sylvie—a sullen girl in her teens with bad skin and torn jeans and a screaming skull on her T-shirt. The first thought that came to Sylvie's exhausted brain was that the pink, girly purse she and Jeff had sent Maeve that last Christmas must not have been at all appreciated. In the picture of the family Jeff had kept on the bookshelf, it was clear that Sean looked just like his father, both fair-skinned, blue-eyed, and Maeve looked like Róisín, darker and tiny to the point of looking almost frail.

But Róisín hadn't been there to pick her up at the airport with the others. On the way back to the house, Conor had chatted on about the unexpected warm weather they'd been having and the sights he thought she might like to see. The houses in the little neighborhoods they drove through had window-boxes and brightly painted doors, like misplaced country cottages. Sylvie loved the sound of the Dublin accent, softer than Jeff used to make it when he imitated it. She loved the round, soft place names on the signs: Fingal, Howth. Sean jumped into the conversation here and there, his voice strangely low and raspy for a young boy. He was full of ideas, asking when they would drive to Dingle or whether they could go around the Ring of Kerry in a coach. Maeve, though, stared silently out the window in the back seat, coughing out angry sighs and glaring at her brother.

At the house in Clontarf, Conor unloaded her luggage and showed her around the place. They had a small backyard with a soccer goal at one end and a view of the Dublin Bay, cold looking and gray under a low sky. They ended the tour in the crowded kitchen and Conor grabbed the electric tea kettle and said, "You'll have a cup then, yeah? You will, of course."

That was when Sylvie registered that Róisín wasn't there. Did she have to work on a Sunday or maybe she'd been out running errands? No one had mentioned her. As tired as she was, Sylvie realized that she hadn't had the common courtesy to ask. "I'm so sorry," she sputtered, "I should have asked before . . . how is Róisín? Did she have to work today? I thought . . ."

Suddenly Maeve barked, "Dad!" and spun around, storming through the swinging kitchen door and slamming up the stairs.

Conor closed his eyes slowly and opened them again. Sylvie could see the strain around them, the wrinkles white like he'd been squinting in the sun. "Let me make you a breakfast, then we'll have a chat."

A half hour later, Conor sat his own full plate across from hers and looked woefully at all she hadn't touched. "You'll starve inside a week if I can't do better than that," he said.

"Oh no! It's good, really! It's just . . . I'm so tired, maybe I should just try to get some sleep."

Conor was already shaking his head. "Ah no," he said, "you can't sleep your first day over or you'll never adjust. You'll be jet-lagged the whole week." He pushed his plate away, sat back in his chair and looked at her. "Sylvie, I didn't tell you before you came because I didn't want you to change your mind, but we've had a bit of a rough go of it here ourselves lately, and that's what has Maeve stirred up."

"Róisín and I," he said, then he sat silent again. "Róisín and I." He shook his head. Sylvie had to lean over the table to hear him, his voice was so soft and his accent so new to her. "We'd been having trouble these few years back now. I never told Jeff so there's no way you'd know. I always thought—the way you do, of course—that we'd work it out in the end. That we'd be right as rain as soon as she left the job in London and found something here, something close. But that didn't happen and then . . . ." Conor looked out into the backyard where Sean was kicking a soccer ball over and over again into the goal. A light rain had begun to fall, but Sean took no notice. He raised his hands in the air and pumped his fists.

Sylvie's mind flashed to the boy she called Martin, the son she and Jeff never had. He'd be about the same age as Sean.

"A few weeks ago she moved out. Moved to London."

Sylvie covered her eyes with her hand. A drumbeat had started in her temples, and she massaged it with her thumb and ring finger. "A few weeks ago?" she repeated.

"I know," Conor said quickly. "I know. I should have told you. That's what has Maeve hotter than a nest of hornets." He looked up at the ceiling. "Maeve wanted me to tell you so you wouldn't come, and then she wants us all to go to London and talk sense to her mother and bring her home."

Sylvie felt his eyes on her, but she couldn't look up. "This was all a mistake," she said. "Let me . . . I'll find a hotel room and . . . I'm going to make arrangements to . . . I should have realized this was a terrible mistake." The tears she was barely holding in scalded her throat. If she left, what would she do? She hadn't planned on driving, and the idea of renting a car and trying to navigate roundabouts on the other side of the road made her feel panicky. What would she do for ten days alone in a strange city?

Conor reached across the table and grabbed her other hand. "No, please. Please don't. I didn't tell you because I wanted you to come."

Sylvie pulled her hand from under his and stood up. She felt dizzy, felt like she might be sick. "Why? Why did you want me to come? How does my being here help anything at all? You don't know me; you'd never even met me before today."

"But we're all grieving," Conor said. "Maybe we can share the grief, and it will be lighter, divide the burden."

The soccer ball grazed the glass door, and Sean ran past in a blur. Sylvie's legs felt weak, and the room seemed to tip. She sat down again. "It's not the same grief," she said. "I'm an intruder into a new routine, a fragile one." She thought of Brian and Regina and their baby, thought she was an intruder there, too. How had she lost the feeling that she belonged anywhere?

SYLVIE HAD IMAGINED being in this kitchen in Dublin when she was booking the trip. Imagining it had gotten her through the school year, through watching Regina buy baby things, through the talks with Brian about what they'd name the baby, helping Regina move into the house she and Jeff had practically picked out for Brian. It was all so odd and awkward. Regina brought paint swatches over one Sunday so Sylvie could help her decide on colors.

When they asked how she was, in that way they did, with that pity in their eyes and the low voice, she'd bring up her trip. The talk would turn to the future, her future, not the baby. The pity evaporated.

And she could spend time dreaming about how the trip would be, looking at pictures of Ireland online—the Cliffs of Moher, the Rock of Cashel—imagining everything. In her mind, the kitchen in Dublin was cozier and dark. In her mind, she sat with Conor and Róisín and they told her funny stories about Jeff that she'd never heard before and they drank tea and ate brown bread with butter and the sweet crackers Jeff had always bought at specialty stores. Biscuits, but not what any American ever thought of as a biscuit. She imagined shopping with Róisín at the open-air markets, dinners with the family at the end of a day where she'd toured the places Jeff had told her about in the city.

She realized too late that she'd come looking for Jeff, for a Jeff she hadn't known and now couldn't know. She closed her eyes and the sudden, overwhelming anger at him felt like a fist closing in her gut. She hated Jeff for romanticizing Ireland, for never taking her there, for dying. She hated that Regina was pregnant. And she was furious at Conor for luring her to Dublin as some sort of international diversion, something to distract from his own home-grown trouble. "This is a mistake," she said.

"How do you know? How do you know it was a mistake? Let it play out. Let it marinate. In a few days, you may be happy you came."

Conor looked up at the ceiling and lowered his voice. "I haven't told Maeve but there's someone else, someone her mother is living with in London. Even if I wanted to, I couldn't pack up the kids and make a little trip to fix this."

"But don't you see," Sylvie said, "that's exactly what I did. I tried to take a trip to fix things, and it won't work. You just said it! It was a mistake and now I've blundered into the middle of the worst time in your life, your *lives*. I don't belong here. Let me . . . let me find a hotel."

"Maybe tomorrow," Conor said. "Stay here with us for a day. Let's see how it goes."


SEAN STOOD BY THE RAILING holding up pieces of bread for the seagulls and pigeons that flapped just beyond his arm's reach. When he threw the bread in the river, the birds swooped and raised a great ruckus of squawking and wings that made him laugh out loud every time.

"He's a happy boy," Sylvie said. Then she was sorry because she saw the anxiety and doubt on Conor's face. He said, "Yeah" on an indrawn breath and Sylvie registered the expression immediately. It was a verbal tic Jeff had told her about, one he said he'd never heard anyone but the Irish do. "They say 'yeah' but it means yes *and* no. It means, *'life's like that and also death.'*" He'd tried to reproduce it for her several times and then given up. "You'll hear it when we go over together," he said, "and you'll know it right away."

She and Conor sat together at a café table on the board-walk. The reflection of the glowing clouds skimmed the gray surface of the Liffy. When the sun broke through, the water threw off chips of golden light that made Sylvie's tired eyes water. She closed them against the brightness, and Conor said, "Ah no, you're doin' grand, sure. Don't close your eyes yet. Just a few more hours and you've made it."

When she opened her eyes, he was smiling at her, and she was too tired to be angry. Conor had walked Sylvie around the city for almost two hours, and she'd been surprised to find that the sometime sunshine, the cool breeze, and the constant movement lifted her spirits some. Sean ran out in front of them to look in the windows of the sporting goods stores or lagged behind to bang a stick against the bars of the ornate iron fences that surrounded some of the houses. Maeve hadn't come along, had remained barricaded in her room. Sylvie had heard Conor from downstairs. The words floating down like seared leaves: "Mom . . . Never . . . Promised." Conor's voice tired and patient, Maeve's, tearful, angry.

Sylvie took another bite of her ham sandwich. The thick white bread, chewy and dense, comforted her. When the sun went in again, Sylvie looked out over the river, at the overturned shopping cart rusting on the far bank, the Guinness can bobbing close below them, a white running shoe marooned in the brown muck. "It's a shame," she said. "Jeff said that the 'Dirty Liffy' has always been a kind of tradition, but you'd think that it would be nicer for everyone to just clean it up."

"Oh, but they have cleaned it," Conor said. "They've been working on it for years now. It's far cleaner than it used to be."

"This is cleaner?" Sylvie swept her hand toward the river just as the sun burst through again.

"Sean," Conor called, "sit over, and eat your sandwich now. You've pestered the birds enough." He turned back to Sylvie and pointed to her sandwich. "You eat, too. That river is cleaner than it ever was. So clean you can swim in it."

Sylvie waited for the wink, and when it didn't come she said, "You can't."

"I did it meself and lived to tell!" Conor said.

"You swam in *that*?"

"Well, you do have to navigate the odd shopping trolley, it's true . . ."

"Did you fall in? What would possess you?"

Sean, who'd been quietly picking the cheese out of his sandwich, piped up. "He did the triathlon. I'm going to do it, too, when I'm old enough."

Sylvie looked back at Conor. "You did? You're a triathlete?" Jeff had done biathlons, cycling and running. He'd been lean, sinewy. Conor wasn't heavy exactly, but he was more comfortably built, and taller with a big, muscled chest and a thicker middle.

"Don't sound so astounded, now. Aren't I a fine athletic specimen if ever you've seen one?" He flexed his bicep. "You like gun shows, do you?"

Sylvie and Sean both started to laugh, and Sean held up his arm, too, flexing and pointing, "I've got a gun show. Look at mine." He pulled the same faux-sexy, serious face as his father.

"Donahue men," Conor said. "No woman can resist."

In the middle of her laughter, Sylvie felt something inside her release, like a dam breaking. Suddenly real laughter bubbled up from underneath layers of grief and pain and anger and exhaustion.

"Now you're having me on," Conor said, "It's not that funny." He put on the sexy face again and she doubled over.

"No, no," Sylvie said, "I'm not laughing at you." But she couldn't stop. "I'm just . . . ." She started laughing again. "I'm tired, I guess. And I haven't laughed . . . I can't remember the last time anyone made me really laugh. I'm so . . ."

Then, without warning, she started to cry. The tears just mixed in, like they'd poured with everything else through the broken wall inside her. She'd read about this. She'd heard people say, "laughing and crying at once," but it had never happened to her. She'd only seen it happen to little children pushed to their limits and she felt suddenly ashamed and out of control. "I'm sorry. I'm sorry." She was coughing through the tears. "I don't know what's come over me."

Sean stood amazed beside her chair and stared at her, fascinated. "Is she mad?" he asked Conor, in a breathless voice.

"Ah no," Conor said. "She's just sad. She's missing your Uncle Jeff, and she's missing home."

Sean put his hand on her arm and patted her and looked at his father. "It's hard," the boy said, "the missing. That's the hard part."

AFTER THEY PAID THE BILL, they walked beside the river again, all the way down past Temple Bar to the Old City Wall. Conor told her that the wall was built in the thirteenth century by the Normans, that it had once surrounded all of Dublin. Sylvie looked at the crumbling remains, the gate standing solid after so long.

It was nearly five-thirty, and yet it still felt like the middle of the afternoon. The earlier breakdown had worn her out. The sun wouldn't set until after ten. Sylvie was so tired that she stumbled twice, and Conor caught her by the elbow.

"We'll go home now," he said, after the second time. "We'll have a little dinner, and you'll sleep. Tomorrow you'll be right as rain."

Sylvie thought of Maeve, imagined her still sulking in the room upstairs, and, tired as she was, she didn't want to go back and face her. In the time that they had walked around the city, Sylvie had begun to dread seeing the girl again. Every time Sylvie thought of Maeve, she thought of her skulking at the top of the stairs; she saw the screaming skull on her T-shirt and her rude, closed, pimply face. Jeff had been her uncle and her godfather. Did she have no feeling for him, for his loss, for Sylvie's loss? She wished Maeve weren't back at the house in Clontarf, poisoning their return, making Sylvie feel mistaken and unwelcome.

Sean was in front of them now, kicking an imaginary soccer ball and whispering like he was announcing the game he played.

"Have you always been athletic, too, running around with a ball all the time, like Sean?" Sylvie switched her purse to the other shoulder and noticed how heavy it was.

"Ah yeah. I was a holy terror like him. Then, you know, with work and the kids and all, I got out of shape. But I'm back at it now. Back in the saddle, as you say over there."

"Is that why you decided to do the triathlon? To get back in shape?"

Conor squinted up at the sun and put his hands in his pockets. He walked beside her for a minute, then said, "It was Jeff, partly. He encouraged me to start running. We'd said we'd do the Dublin marathon together. We'd made a pact. But after he died, I couldn't see doing that race. Plus, I like that in a triathlon I could be mediocre at everything and still finish."

Sylvie smiled, "He used to try to get me to run, too. It was kind of a religion for him, and he wanted converts." When had she last run? Had she run since his death? She realized with a start that she hadn't, that she wouldn't ever have to run again. It was a strange relief. Jeff had always been loudly quiet when she said she was going out for a run and changed her mind. When she ran with him, he ran way out in front and then circled back because she was so slow. Sometimes he'd run with her and then go out for another run afterward. It all felt like a judgment, felt like so much pressure.

"It was Róisín, too," Conor said, more softly. "I wanted to show her that I could be driven. I could be, you know, manly. It didn't work in the end anyway, but I took a shot at it, you know like." He smiled a sad smile.

WHEN THEY OPENED the door to the house, Maeve came flying out of the kitchen like she'd been surprised at their arrival, and she flounced by them and flew up the stairs in a renewal of her former rage. It was meant to seem like happenstance, but Sylvie had the feeling that Maeve had been waiting in the kitchen, listening for the car doors. Sylvie remembered planning things like this herself when she was Maeve's age.

It took Conor a couple of beats to recover himself and become Maeve's father, and then he started up the steps behind her in big strides, saying her name. Maeve slammed the bedroom door, and Conor opened it and slammed it again.

Sylvie looked over at Sean who stood beside her looking up the stairs after his father and sister.

"She gets like this," he said.

Sylvie smiled over at him. "Often?"

"Ah, she's alright most of the time." Sean turned and headed toward the little living room across from the stairs. "You wouldn't want to play a video game, no?"

"I'll watch you," she said. But as soon as she sat on the couch, she closed her eyes.

She didn't know how long she'd been asleep when someone touched her shoulder. For just a second, she couldn't remember where she was, who these people were, and then it all came back. Maeve stood in front of her, red-faced and teary.

Conor said. "Maeve, what do you have to say?"

"I'm sorry, Aunt Sylvie," she whispered, her voice thick and her eyes down.

*Aunt Sylvie.* The words stopped her breath. No one had ever called her that.

"And what are you sorry for?" Maeve's father prompted.

*That's who I'll be to the new baby*, Sylvie thought, and for the first time she pictured herself holding the baby, looking into a tiny, new face. A baby that might have Jeff's nose or eyes as she realized for the first time, Maeve did. She looked hard at the girl's face and suddenly saw the family resemblance she had missed before.

And then Maeve broke free from her father's grasp and launched herself forward into Sylvie's lap, her wet face on Sylvie's chest, her hipbone pressing into Sylvie's middle. Sylvie raised her hands above the girl and looked at Conor, whose face mirrored her own surprise and confusion.

"It's alright, honey," Sylvie said, and she smoothed the brown tangle of the girl's hair. Maeve was all angles, elbows and knees. Sylvie pulled her chin back to look down at the half-hidden profile, the pimply skin, the tiny silver snowflake earring. "It's alright," she said, again. "It's all going to be okay. You'll see." Maeve held her, breathing hard with the left-over tears; every now and then a high-pitched sob escaped.

Sylvie closed her eyes and breathed in. Maeve smelled like Juicy Fruit gum and shampoo, and the girl's weight pushing her into the soft cushions of the couch made Sylvie feel oddly real, rooted in her own body in a way that she couldn't remember feeling before. She thought again of running, Jeff saying that running had made him feel his life. She'd never completely understood it before. She wondered if this was what he'd felt—connected to a pulse inside and beyond him. She ran her hand up the girl's thin back, felt the rhythm of her spine.

She imagined Jeff and Conor running side by side in that long race they wouldn't ever run together. How strange bodies were. How each cell carries a pattern that passes along over and over again. She felt her body yielding under Maeve's, but also lifting, rising. She was here—here in this moment, in this embrace, here in Ireland. The thought made her smile, and then, she had to suppress an astonished laugh. She'd done it. She had gotten on a plane alone and gone somewhere she'd never been before for the first time in her life. She'd gotten through the difficult day, through the awful year. Suddenly, Sylvie felt strong. She closed her eyes to focus on the feeling, to pull herself into the moment, to breathe in time with the girl who held her.

"Aunt Sylvie," Maeve said again, a damp breath in the hollow of her collar bone.

*Aunt Sylvie.* She felt the words settle inside her. This is who she would be, who she was now to Maeve and Sean, who she'd be to the new baby. She would be someone new. Someone Jeff had never known. All the days stretching before her flooded with new grief and possibility.

# BIKES

I. When Jeff was ten, he'd ride to the top of the cul-del-sac on the blue Schwinn he'd come to think of as a "kid's bike," and he'd watch them from a distance. He had wanted the BMX for two years before his mother gave him one the Christmas he was eleven years old. It was the same year his father left.

The older boys who rode at the end of the cul-de-sac could do all kinds of tricks: bar spins, bunny hops, even wall rides. When they saw his new bike, one called, "Sweet ride."

Afternoons, he rode for hours, the bike rising under him. The shouting faces of the older boys blurring together with the white fronts of the houses, the gray concrete beneath him. Voices lifted as he levitated the spinning bike, but he heard only the silence beneath the sound, the silence beneath his breath.

When he hit the ground again, he felt like his world had changed. He had flown; he would fly again.

His memory of the bike would always be this—joy, power, speed. Though he knew he'd fallen often, even had scars on his knees and elbows, a long red line that ran up the side of his calf, he couldn't remember pain or even fear.

It was always fall and he'd always just gotten off the bus from middle school, the weather perpetually crisp and bright, an eternity of late afternoon light.

II.  He'd ridden the BMX on and off through high school, but it wasn't the same. He wasn't the same. There were classes and girls and parties. Beer and whiskey, sex, a little pot. The bike leaned against the wall of the garage.

Loading up the car to move him to campus, his mother had pointed at it, and he shook his head. He didn't even look where she pointed.

In college, Jeff took up running.

He liked the rhythm of his footfall; he liked being inside his own breathing. He liked the satisfied, finished feeling at the end when his breath rifled through him, and his legs burned.

III.  At 33, he found bikes again.

Later, Sylvie would tease him that he'd caved to peer pressure a second time, and though he laughed it off, he knew, too, that if it weren't for seeing the "bike dude" fly by him on the Pinarello as he ran along the shoulder of the road, he might never have reignited his love for cycling.

Jeff and the bike dude passed each other every morning at more or less the same time and waved. One day Jeff called, "Sweet ride." The guy stopped and said, "Hey, do you ever ride? Do you want to?"

"How old is he?" Sylvie asked.

"He's ageless," Jeff said. "His face looks like it's carved from obsidian."

Sylvie rolled her eyes.

"I swear to you. He's got this dark skin, and as he blows by me, the muscles on his calves look like . . . he's some kind of god."

"So, you're going to ride with these *gods*?" Sylvie said. "You're going to buy a bike and ride with the gods."

IV.   Memento Mori

I burst free from the one dense point I had thought myself to be
Carrying the images that had become me
had become gravity
the lipstick print on white tissues in my mother's purse
the weight of Bowtie on the bottom of our bed
the whorled shell of a mud snail in Brian's hand
dark energy—a decimal point, 122 zeroes, a one
sledding with Regina when we were kids
Sylvie in a white dress in a hot church
roar and silence and roar as I ducked under an ocean wave
the blue BMX, sweet ride

# ACKNOWLEDGMENTS

The following stories first appeared in these periodicals:

"Taking Care," *Blue Lake Review*

"Explain," *Bellevue Literary Review*

"Nine Months," *Superstition Review*

"Breaking In," *Forge*

"Sympathy," *The Valley Review*

* * *

Because my father, Tom Colwell, was a hospital administrator, I grew up volunteering for, working in, and hanging around hospitals, and I came to understand how fundamental they are to the communities they serve. Beebe Hospital, at the center of these stories, is a real hospital that has served the Delaware communities of Lewes and Rehoboth since 1916. I am grateful to Beebe and to the two hospitals where my father worked, St. Francis Hospital in Delaware and Crozer Chester Medical Center in Pennsylvania.

More importantly, I am deeply grateful to all the health care workers and first responders who serve our communities every day, giving us their compassion, talent, effort, and expertise. Several health care workers and first responders helped me with this book, directly or indirectly, including Jeff Fried, Holly Deihl, and James Priano. My son, Thomas Keegan, worked as a first responder, and I'm grateful to him for his compassion and bravery and for giving me perspective about being the one who runs into situations that everyone else is running away from.

*Broken Heart Syndrome* explores how a close-knit community processes and heals after a loss, so I owe a debt of gratitude to several community institutions:

- Thank you to the Sussex Family YMCA and the Navy Seal Bootcamp Class for bringing together so many people who helped inspire this book.

- Thank you to my students and colleagues at the University of Delaware Associate in Arts Program in Georgetown, Delaware, where I'm privileged to read and work with amazing writers every semester.

- Thank you to the Rehoboth Beach Writers Guild, the most supportive community of readers and writers anyone could ask for.

Thank you to publisher Dr. Ross Tangedal and the whole amazing team at Cornerstone Press, including Ava Willett (in media), and Sophie McPherson, Autumn Vine, and Madison Schultz (in sales). I want to give special thanks to senior editor Ellie Atkinson for her dedicated readings and re-readings and her careful comments. I feel so fortunate to be part of the Legacy Series.

I could write nothing without the support and love of my family: Jeanne Colwell Iasella, and her husband Gino; my nieces, Anna and Francesca; my brothers, Thomas and James Colwell; my son, Thomas Keegan, his wife, Alyssa; my grandson, Ciaran James; and my stepmother, Louise Colwell.

I am forever grateful to my husband, James Keegan, for his constant support, unfailing encouragement, and love. I'm grateful for our years of one days.

There would be no book without my writing partner and dear friend, Maribeth Fischer. In the twenty years that we have met once a week to discuss our work, she has read every word of every draft of every story I've written. Her intelligence, ear for language, intuitive understanding of character, and compassionate comments keep me writing when I would have long ago given up. She walks into the imaginative world of the story with me and helps me to know what I know, and to honor and be patient with what I don't yet know. She is here on every page, and I'm so grateful.

ANNE COLWELL is the author of the poetry books *Believing Their Shadows* (2010) and *Mother's Maiden Name* (2013). Her work has appeared in numerous journals, including *Bellevue Literary Review, California Quarterly, Southern Poetry Review, and The Madison Review,* and she is the recipient of fellowships from the Delaware State Arts Council, the Virginia Center for the Creative Arts, and the Bread Loaf Writers Conference. She is a professor of English at the University of Delaware.